"What exactly [are you] proposing with this press conference and by bringing me back to Isle Saint Croix?

"That's assuming I'll agree to go," she added quickly.

Alix looked at Leila. She was pale and even more beautiful than he remembered. Were her eyes always that big? The moment he'd seen her standing in the foyer, his blood had leaped as if injected by currents of pure electricity.

"You'll come because you're carrying my heir and the whole world knows it now."

Leila looked hunted, her arms crossed tightly over her chest again, pushing the swells of those luscious breasts up. The thought of Leila's body ripening with his seed, his child, gave him another shockingly sudden jolt of lust.

Leila was pacing now. "What is the solution here? There has to be a solution..." She stopped and faced him again. "I mean, it's not as if you're really intending to marry me. The engagement is just for show until things die down again, right?"

She looked so hopeful Alix almost felt sorry for her. Almost. Her reluctance to marry him caught at him somewhere very primal and possessive.

"No, Leila. We will be getting married. In two weeks."

One Night With Consequences

When one night...leads to pregnancy!

When succumbing to a night of unbridled desire
it's impossible to think past the morning after!

But, with the sheets barely settled,
that little blue line appears on the pregnancy test
and it doesn't take long to realize that
one night of white-hot passion has turned into
a lifetime of consequences!

Only one question remains:

How do you tell a man you've just met that you're
about to share more than just his bed?

Find out in:

More stories in the
One Night With Consequences series
can be found at Harlequin.com

Abby Green

An Heir Fit for a King

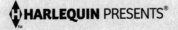
HARLEQUIN PRESENTS®

ISBN-13: 978-0-373-13376-5

An Heir Fit for a King

First North American Publication 2015

Recycling programs for this product may not exist in your area.

This edition published by arrangement with Harlequin Books S.A.

For questions and comments about the quality of this book, please contact us at CustomerService@Harlequin.com.

Printed in U.S.A.

www.Harlequin.com

Irish author **Abby Green** threw in a very glamorous career in film and TV—which really consisted of a lot of standing in the rain outside actors' trailers—to pursue her love of romance. After she'd bombarded Harlequin with manuscripts they kindly accepted one, and an author was born. She lives in Dublin, Ireland, and loves any excuse for distraction. Visit her at abby-green.com or email abbygreenauthor@gmail.com.

Books by Abby Green

Harlequin Presents

Forgiven but not Forgotten?
Exquisite Revenge
One Night with the Enemy
The Legend of de Marco
The Call of the Desert
The Sultan's Choice
Secrets of the Oasis
In Christofides' Keeping
The Virgin's Secret

The Chatsfield

Delucca's Marriage Contract

Billionaire Brothers

The Bride Fonseca Needs
Fonseca's Fury

Blood Brothers

When Falcone's World Stops Turning
When Christakos Meets His Match
When Da Silva Breaks the Rules

Visit the Author Profile page
at Harlequin.com for more titles.

This is for Sheila Hodgson...
thanks for your support and calming influence
while life got seriously in the way of this book!

I'd also like to thank the beautiful stranger
working in the perfume shop in the Westbury Mall
in Dublin, who sparked the original idea for this
story, and a very special thanks to Penny Ellis of
Floris, London, who gave me my first experience
in how to build a perfume.
Any glaring errors are purely my own!

CHAPTER ONE

LEILA VERUGHESE WAS just wondering morosely to herself what would happen when her dwindling supplies of perfume ran out completely when out of the corner of her eye she spotted something and turned to look, glad of the distraction to her maudlin thoughts.

It was a sleek black car, pulled up outside her small House of Leila perfume shop. The shop she'd inherited from her mother, on the Place Vendôme in Paris. When she took a closer look she saw a veritable *fleet* of sleek black cars. The lead one had flags flying on the bonnet, but Leila couldn't make out what country they were from—even though she'd spent most of her life identifying the glamorous comings and goings from the exclusive Ritz Hotel across the square.

A man hopped out of the front of the car, clearly a bodyguard of some sort, with an earpiece in his ear. He looked around before opening the back door and Leila's eyes widened when she saw who emerged. As if they had to widen purely to be able to take him in better.

It was a man—unmistakably and unashamedly a man. Which was a ridiculous thing to think… One was either a man or a woman, after all. But it was as if his very masculinity reached out before him like a crackling energy. He uncoiled to a height well over six feet, towering over the smaller, blockier man beside him. Powerfully built, with broad shoulders in a long black overcoat.

He looked as if he was about to come towards Leila's shop when he stopped suddenly, and Leila saw a moment of irritation cross his face before he turned back to talk to someone who had to be in the back of the car. A wife? A girlfriend? He went and put a big hand on the roof of the car as he consulted the person inside.

Leila caught a glimpse of a long length of bare toned thigh and a flash of blonde hair and then the man straightened again and began striding towards the shop, flanked by his minders.

It was only now that Leila even registered his face. She'd never seen anything so boldly beautiful in all her life. Dark olive skin—dark enough to be Arabic? High cheekbones and a sensual mouth. It might have been pretty if it hadn't been for the deep-set eyes, strong brows and even stronger jaw, which had clenched now, along with that look of irritation.

He had short hair—dark, cut close to his skull. Which had that same beautiful masculine shape as his face.

Shock held Leila still for a long moment as he got closer and closer. For a second, just before the shop door opened, his eyes caught hers and she had the strangest notion of a huge sleek bird of prey, swooping down to pick her up in his talons and carry her away.

The dark-haired shop assistant behind the glass of the shop barely impinged on Alix Saint Croix's consciousness as he strode to the door. *Surprise me.* His mouth tightened. If he'd been able to say that the previous night had been…pleasurable, he might have been more inclined to 'surprise' his lover. He was a man who was not used to obeying the demands of anyone else, and the only reason he was indulging Carmen's sudden whim for perfume was because he was all too eager to get away from her.

She'd arrived in his suite the previous evening, and their subsequent lovemaking had been...*adequate*. Alix had found himself wondering when was the last time he'd been so consumed with lust or by a woman that he'd lost his mind in pleasure? *Never*, a little voice had whispered as his lover had sauntered from the bed to the bathroom, making sure all her assets were displayed to best advantage.

Alix had been bored. And, because women seemed to have a seventh sense designed purely to detect that, his lover had become very uncharacteristically compliant and sweet. So much so that it had set Alix's teeth on edge. And after a day of watching waif-thin models prancing up and down a catwalk he was even more on edge.

But, as his advisor had pointed out when he'd grumbled to him on the phone earlier, 'This is good, Alix. It's helping us lull them into a false sense of security: they believe you have nothing on your agenda but the usual round of socialising and modelising.'

Alix did not like being considered a *modeliser*, and he pushed open the door to the shop with more force than was necessary, finally registering the shop assistant who was looking at him with a mixture of shock and awe on her face.

He also registered within the same nanosecond that she was the most beautiful woman he'd ever seen in his life.

The door shut behind him, a small bell tinkling melodically, but he didn't notice. She had pale olive skin, a straight nose and full soft lips. *Sexy*. A firm, yet delicate jaw. High cheekbones. Her hair was a sleek fall of black satin behind her shoulders and Alix had the bizarre compulsion to reach out and see if it would slip through his fingers like silk.

But it was her eyes that floored him... They were huge light emerald gems with the longest black lashes, framed by gracefully arched black brows. She looked like a Far Eastern princess.

'Who are you?'

Was that his voice? It sounded like a croak. Stunned. There was an instant fire kindling in his belly and his blood. The fire he'd lamented the lack of last night. It was as if his body was ahead of his brain in terms of absorbing her beauty.

She blinked and those long lashes veiled her stunning eyes for a moment.

'I'm the owner of the shop, Leila Verughese.'

The name suited her. Exotic. Alix somehow found the necessary motor skills to put out his hand. 'Alix Saint Croix.'

Recognition flashed in her eyes, unmistakable. She flushed, her cheeks going a pretty shade of pink and Alix surmised cynically that of *course* she'd heard of him. Who hadn't?

Her hand slipped into his then, small and delicate, cool, and the effect was like a rocket launching deep inside Alix. His blood boiled and his hand tightened reflexively around hers.

He struggled to make sense of this immediate and extreme physical and mental reaction. He was used to seeing a woman and assessing her from a distance, his desires firmly under control. This woman... *Leila*...was undeniably beautiful, yes. But she was dressed like a pharmacist, with a white coat over a very plain blue shirt and black trousers. Even in flat shoes, though, she was relatively tall, reaching his shoulder. He found himself imagining her in spindly high heels, how close her mouth would be if he wanted to just bend down slightly...

She took her hand back and Alix blinked.

'You are looking for a perfume?'

Alix's brain felt sluggish. Perfume? Why was he looking for perfume? *Carmen*. Waiting for him in the car. Immediately he scowled again, and the woman in front of him took a step back.

He put out a hand. 'Sorry, no...' He cursed silently—what was wrong with him? 'That is, *yes*, I'm looking for a perfume. For someone.'

The woman looked at him. 'Do you have any particular scent in mind?'

Alix dragged his gaze from her with an effort and looked around the small shop for the first time. Each wall was mirrored glass, with glass shelves and counters. Glass and gold perfume bottles covered the surfaces, giving the space a golden hue.

The decor was opulent without being stifling. And there wasn't the stench of overpowering perfume that Alix would normally associate with a shop like this. The ambience was cool, calm. Serene. Like her. He realised that she exuded a sense of calm and that he was reacting to that as well.

Almost absently he said, 'I'm looking for a scent for my mistress.'

When there was no immediate reaction such as Alix was used to—he said what he wanted and people jumped—he looked at the woman. Her mouth was pursed and an unmistakable air of disapproval was being directed at him. Intriguing. No one ever showed Alix their true reactions.

He arched a brow. 'You have a problem with that?'

To his further fascination her cheeks coloured and she

looked away. Then she said stiffly, 'It's not for me to say what's an appropriate term for your...partner.'

Leila cursed herself for showing her reaction and moved away to one of the walls of shelves, as if to seek out some perfume samples.

Her father had once offered the role of mistress to Leila's mother—*after* she'd given birth to their illegitimate daughter. He'd seduced Deepika Verughese when he'd been doing business in India with Leila's grandfather, but had then turned his back on her when she'd arrived in Paris, disgraced and pregnant, all the way from Jaipur.

Her mother had declined his offer to become his kept woman, too proud and bitter after his initial rejection, and had told Leila the story while pointing out all the kept women of the various famous people and dignitaries who'd come into the shop over the years, as a salutary lesson in what women were prepared to do to feather their nests.

Leila's mind cleared of the painful memory. She hated it that she'd reacted so unprofessionally just now, but before she could say anything else she heard the man move and looked up into the glass to see him coming closer. He looked even larger reflected in the mirror, with his dark image being sent back a hundred times.

She realised that his eyes were a very dark grey.

'You know who I am?'

She nodded. She'd known who he was as soon as he'd said his name. He was the infamous exiled King of a small island kingdom off the coast of North Africa, near Southern Spain. He was a renowned financial genius, with fingers in almost every business one could think of—including most recently an astronomical investment in the new oil fields of Burquat in the Middle East.

There were rumours that he was going to make a claim

on his throne, but if this visit was anything to go by he was concerned with nothing more than buying trinkets for his lover. And she had no idea why that made her feel so irritable.

Alix Saint Croix continued. 'So you'll know that a man like me doesn't have girlfriends or partners. I take mistresses. Women who know what to expect and don't expect anything more.'

Something hardened inside her. She knew all about men like him. Unfortunately. And the evidence of this man's single-minded, cynical nature made her see red. It made her sick, because it reminded her of her own naivety in the face of overwhelming evidence that what she sought didn't exist.

Nevertheless she was determined not to let this man draw her down another painful memory lane. She crossed her arms over her chest. 'Not all women are as cynical as you make out.'

Something hard crossed his face. 'The women who move in my circles are.'

'Well, maybe your circles are too small?'

She couldn't believe the words tripping out of her mouth, but he'd pushed a button—a very sensitive button. She almost expected him to storm out of her shop, but to her surprise Alix Saint Croix's mouth quirked on one side, making him look even sexier. Dangerous.

'Perhaps they are, indeed.'

Leila suddenly felt hot and claustrophobic. He was looking at her too intensely, and then his gaze dropped to where the swells of her breasts were pushed up by her crossed arms. She took them down hurriedly and reached for the nearest bottle of perfume, only half registering the label.

She thrust it towards him. 'This is one of our most

popular scents. It's floral-based with a hint of citrus. It's light and zesty—perfect for casual wear.'

Alix Saint Croix shook his head. 'No, I don't think that'll do. I want something much earthier. Sensuous.'

Leila put down the bottle with a clatter and reached for another bottle. 'This might be more appropriate, then. It's got fruity top notes, but a woody, musky base.'

He cocked his head and said consideringly, 'It's so hard to know unless you can smell it.'

Leila's shirt felt too tight. She wanted to undo a top button. What was wrong with her?

She turned back to the counter and took a smelling strip out of a jar, ready to spray it so that he could smell it. And go. She wanted him gone. He was too disturbing to her usually very placid equilibrium.

But before she could spray, a large hand wrapped around her arm, stopping her.

Heat zinged straight to her belly. She looked up at him.

'Not on a piece of paper. I think you'd agree that a scent has to be on the skin to be best presented?'

Feeling slightly drugged and stupid, Leila said, 'It's a woman's scent.'

He cocked a brow again. 'So spray some on your wrist and I'll smell it.'

The shock that reverberated through Leila was as if he'd just said *Take off all your clothes, please.*

She had to struggle to compose herself, get a grip. She'd often sprayed perfume on her own skin so that someone could get a fuller sense of it. But this man had made the request sound almost indecent.

Praying that her hand wouldn't shake, Leila took the top off the bottle and pulled up her sleeve to spray some of the scent. When the liquid hit the underside of her wrist she shivered slightly. It felt absurdly sensual all of a sudden.

Alix Saint Croix still had a hand wrapped around her arm and now he moved it down to take the back of her hand in his, wrapping long fingers around hers. He moved his head down to smell the perfume, his dark head coming close to her breast.

But he kept his eyes on her, and from this close she could see lighter flecks of grey, like silver mercury. Leila's breath stopped when she felt his breath feather along her skin. Those lips were far too close to the centre of her palm, which was clammy.

He seemed to consider the scent until Leila's nerves twanged painfully. Her belly was a contracted ball of nerves.

A movement over his head caught her eye and she saw a sleek, tall blonde emerge from the back of the car with a phone clamped to her ear. She was wearing an indecently tight, slinky dress and a ridiculously ineffectual jacket for the cool autumn weather.

He must have picked up on her distraction and straightened to look out of the window too. Leila noticed a tension come into his body as his girlfriend—*mistress*—saw him and gesticulated with clear irritation, all while still talking on the phone.

'Your…er…mistress is waiting for you.' Leila's voice felt scratchy.

He still had his hand wrapped around hers and now let her go. Leila tucked it well out of reach.

He morphed before her eyes into someone much cooler, indecipherable. Perversely, it didn't comfort her.

'I'll take it.'

Leila blinked at him.

'The perfume,' he expanded, and for a moment a glint of what they'd just shared made his eyes flash.

Leila jerked into action. 'Of course. It'll only take me a moment to package it up.'

She moved to get a bag and paper and quickly and inexpertly packaged up the perfume, losing all of her customary cool. When she had it ready she handed it over and avoided his eye. A wad of cash landed on the counter but Leila wasn't about to check it.

And then, without another word, he turned around and strode out again, catching his...whatever she was...by the arm and hustling her back into the car.

His scent lingered on the air behind him, and in a very delayed reaction Leila assimilated the various components with an expertise that was like a sixth sense—along with the realisation that his scent had impacted on her as soon as he'd walked in, on a level that wasn't rational. Someplace else. Somewhere she wasn't used to scents impacting.

It was a visceral reaction. Primal. His scent was clean, with a hint of something very *male* that most certainly hadn't come out of a bottle. The kind of evocative scent that would make someone a fortune if they could bottle it: the pure essence of a virile male in his prime. Earthy. Musky.

A pulse between Leila's legs throbbed and she pressed her thighs together, horrified.

What was wrong with her? The man was a *king*, for God's sake, and he had a mistress that he was unashamed about. She should be thinking *good riddance*, but what she was thinking was much more confused.

It made alarm bells ring. It reminded her of another man who had come into the shop and who had very skilfully set about wooing her—only to turn into a nasty stranger when he'd realised that Leila had no intention of giving him what he wanted...which had been very far removed from what *Leila* had wanted.

She looked stupidly at the money on the counter for a moment, before realising that he'd vastly overpaid her for the perfume, but all she could think about was that last enigmatic look he'd shot her, just before he'd ducked into the car—a look that had seemed to say he'd be back. And soon.

And in light of their conversation, and the way he'd made her feel, Leila knew she shouldn't be remotely intrigued. But she was. And not even the ghost of memories past could stop it.

A little later, after Leila had locked up and gone upstairs to the small flat she'd shared with her mother all her life, she found herself gravitating to the window, which looked out over the Place Vendôme. The opera glasses that her mother had used for years to check out the comings and goings at the Ritz were sitting nearby, and for a second Leila felt an intense pang of grief for her mother.

Leila pushed aside the past and picked up the glasses and looked through them, seeing the usual flurry of activity when someone arrived at the hotel in a flash car. She tilted the glasses upwards to where the rooms were— and her whole body froze when she caught a glimpse of a familiar masculine figure against a brightly lit opulent room.

She trained the glasses on the sight, hating herself for it but unable to look away. It was him. Alix Saint Croix. The overcoat was gone. And the jacket. He had his back to her and was dressed in a waistcoat and shirt and trousers. Hands in his pockets were drawing the material of his trousers over his very taut and muscular backside.

Instantly Leila felt damp heat coil down below and squeezed her legs together.

He was looking at something in front of him, and Leila

tensed even more when the woman he'd been with came into her line of vision. She'd taken off the jacket and the flimsy dress was now all she wore. Her body was as sleek and toned as a throughbred horse. Leila vaguely recognised her as a world-famous lingerie model.

She could see that she held something in her hand, and when it glinted she realised it was the bottle of perfume. The woman sprayed it on her wrist and lifted it to smell, a sexy smile curling her wide mouth upwards.

She sprayed more over herself and Leila winced slightly. The trick with perfume was always *less is more*. And then she threw the bottle aside, presumably to a nearby chair or couch, and proceeded to pull down the skinny straps of her dress. Then she peeled the top half of her dress down, exposing small but perfect breasts.

Leila gasped at the woman's confidence. She'd never have the nerve to strip in that way in front of a man.

And then Alix Saint Croix moved. He turned away from the woman and walked to the window. For a second he loomed large in Leila's glasses, filling them with that hard-boned face. He looked intent. And then he pulled a drape across, obscuring the view, almost as if he'd known Leila was watching from across the square like a Peeping Tom.

Disgusted with herself, Leila threw the glasses down and got up to pace in her small apartment. She berated herself. *How* could a man like that even capture her attention? He was exactly what her mother had warned her about: rich and arrogant. Not even prepared to see women as anything other than mistresses, undoubtedly interchanged with alarming frequency once the novelty with each one had worn off.

Leila had already refused to take her mother's warnings to heart once, and had suffered a painful blow to her confidence and pride because of it.

Full of pent-up energy, she dragged on a jacket and went outside for a brisk walk around the nearby Tuileries gardens, telling herself over and over again first of all that nothing had happened with Alix Saint Croix in her shop that day, secondly that she'd never see him again, and thirdly that she didn't care.

The following evening dusk was falling as Leila went to lock the front door of her shop. It had been a long day, with only a trickle of customers and two measly sales. Thanks to the recession, niche businesses everywhere had taken a nosedive, and since the factory that manufactured the House of Leila scents had closed down she hadn't had the funds to seek out a new factory.

She'd been reduced to selling off the stock she had left in the hope that enough sales would give her the funds to start making perfumes again.

She was just about to turn the lock when she looked up through the glass to see a familiar tall dark figure, flanked by a couple of other men, approaching her door. The almost violent effect on her body of seeing him in the flesh again mocked her for fooling herself that she'd managed not to think about him all day.

The exiled King with the tragic past.

Leila had looked him up on the Internet last night in a moment of weakness and had read about how his parents and younger brother had been slaughtered during a military coup. The fact that he'd escaped to live in exile had become something of a legend.

Her immediate instinct was to lock the door and pull the blind down—fast. But he was right outside now and looking at her. The faintest glimmer of a smile touched his mouth. She could see a day's worth of stubble shadowing his jaw.

Obeying professional reflexes rather than her instincts, Leila opened the door and stepped back. He came in and once again it was as if her brain was slowing to a halt. It was consumed with taking note of his sheer masculine beauty.

Determined not to let him rattle her again, Leila assumed a polite, professional mask. 'How did your mistress like the perfume?'

A lurid image of the woman putting on that striptease threatened to undo Leila's composure but she pushed it out of her head with effort.

Alix Saint Croix made an almost dismissive gesture with his hand. 'She liked it fine. That's not why I'm here.'

Leila found it hard to draw in a breath. Suddenly terrified of why he *was* there, she gabbled, 'By the way, you left far too much money for the perfume.'

She turned and went to the counter and took out an envelope containing the excess he'd paid. She'd been intending to drop it to the hotel for him, but hadn't had the nerve all day. She held it out now.

Alix barely looked at it. He speared her with that grey gaze and said, 'I want to take you out to dinner.'

Panic fluttered in Leila's gut and her hand tightened on the envelope, crushing it. 'What did you say?'

He pushed open his light overcoat to put his hands in his pockets, drawing attention to another pristine three-piece suit, lovingly moulded to muscles that did not belong to an urban civilised man, more to a warrior.

'I said I would like you to join me for dinner.'

Leila frowned. 'But you have a mistress.'

Something stern crossed Alix Saint Croix's face and the grey in his eyes turned to steel. 'She is no longer my mistress.'

Leila recalled what she'd seen the previous night and

blurted out, 'But I saw you—you were together—' She stopped and couldn't curb the heat rising. The last thing she wanted was for him to know she'd been spying, and she said quickly, 'She certainly seemed to be under the impression that you were together.'

She hoped he'd assume she was referring to when she'd seen the woman waiting for him outside the shop.

Alix's face was indecipherable. 'As I said, we are no longer together.'

Leila felt desperate. And disgusted. And disappointed, which was even worse. Of course a man like him would interchange his women without breaking a sweat.

'But I don't even know you—you're a total stranger.'

His mouth twitched slightly. 'Which could be helped by sharing conversation over dinner, *non*?'

Leila had a very strong urge to back away, but forced herself to stand her ground. She was in *her* shop. *Her* space. And everything in her screamed at her to resist this man. He was too gorgeous, too big, too smooth, too famous...too much.

Something reckless gripped her and she blurted out, 'I saw you. The two of you... I didn't intend to, but when I looked out of my window last night I saw you in your room. With her. She was taking off her clothes...'

Leila willed down the embarrassed heat and tilted up her chin defiantly. She didn't care if he thought she was some kind of stalker.

His gaze narrowed on her. 'I saw you too...across the square, silhouetted in your window.'

Now she blanched. 'You did?'

He nodded. 'It merely confirmed that I wanted you. And not her.'

Leila was caught, trapped in his gaze and in his own confession. 'You pulled the curtain across. For privacy.'

His mouth firmed. 'Yes. For privacy while I asked her to put her dress back on and get out, because the relationship was over.'

Leila shivered at his coolness. 'But that's so cruel. You'd just bought her a gift.'

Something infinitely cynical lit those grey eyes and Leila hated it.

'Believe me, a woman like Carmen is no soft-centred fool with notions of where the relationship was going. She knew it was finite. The relationship was ending whether I'd met you or not.'

Leila balked. She definitely veered more towards the *soft-centred fool* end of the scale.

She folded her arms and fought the pull from her gut to follow him blindly. She'd done that with a man once before, with her stupid, vulnerable heart on her sleeve. It made her hard now. 'Thank you for the invitation, but I'm afraid I must say no.'

His brows snapped together in a frown. 'Are you married?'

His gaze dropped to her left hand as if to look for a ring, and something flashed in his eyes when he took in her ringless fingers. Leila's hands curled tight. Too late.

The personal question told her she was doing the right thing and she said frostily, 'That is none of your business, sir. I'd like you to leave.'

For a tiny moment Alix Saint Croix's eyes widened on her, and then he said coolly, 'Very well, I'm sorry for disturbing you. Good evening, Miss Verughese.'

CHAPTER TWO

ALIX WAS HALFWAY across the quiet square, fuelled by a surge of angry disbelief, before the thought managed to break through: no woman, *ever*, had turned him down like that. So summarily. Coldly. As if he'd overstepped some invisible mark on the ground. As if he was...*beneath* her.

He dismissed his security detail with a flick of his hand as he walked into the hotel, with staff scurrying in his wake, the elevator attendant jumping to attention. Alix ignored them all, his mind filled with incredulity that she had said *no*.

He'd ended his liaison with Carmen specifically to pursue Leila Verughese.

When Carmen had undressed in front of him in his suite he'd felt nothing but impatience to see her gone. And then, when he'd gone to his window and seen the light shining from a small window above the perfume shop and that slim figure, all he'd seen was *her* alluring body in his mind's eye. The hint of generous curves told of a very classic feminine shape—not exactly fashion-forward, like Carmen, with tiny breasts and an almost androgynous figure, but all the more alluring for that.

He wanted her with a hunger he hadn't allowed himself to feel in a long time. And that impatience to see Carmen gone had become a compelling need.

When Alix got to his suite of rooms he threw off his coat and prowled like a restless animal. He felt animalistic.

How *dared* she turn him down? He wanted her. The exotic princess who sold perfume.

Why did he want her so badly?

The question pricked at him like a tiny barb and he couldn't ignore it. He'd only ever wanted one other woman in a similar way. A woman who had made him think she was different from all the others. When she'd been even worse.

Alix, young and far more naive than he'd ever wanted to admit at the age of eighteen, had been seduced by a beautiful body and an act of innocence honed to perfection.

Until he'd walked into her college rooms one day and seen one of his own bodyguards thrusting between her pale legs. The image was clear enough to mock him. Years later.

As if his own parents' toxic marriage hadn't already drummed it into him that men and women together brought pain and disharmony.

Ever since then Alix had excised all emotion where women were concerned. They were mistresses—who pleasured him and accompanied him to social events. Until the time came for him to choose a wife who would be his Queen. And then his marriage would be different. It wouldn't be toxic. It would be harmonious and respectful.

Alix thought about that now. Because that time would be coming soon. He was already being presented with prospective wives to choose from. Princesses from different principalities who all looked dismayingly like horses. But Alix didn't care. His wife would be his consort, adept at dealing with the social aspects of her role and providing him with heirs.

So why is this woman getting under your skin?

She's not, he affirmed to himself.

She was just a stunningly beautiful woman who'd connected with him on some very base level and he wasn't used to that.

Alix didn't like to recall that first meeting, when just seeing her had been like a defibrillator shocking him back to life.

His was a life that needed no major distractions right now. He had enough going on with the very real prospect that in a couple of weeks he was going to regain control of his throne. Something he'd been working towards all his life.

And yet this woman was lingering in his mind, compelling him to make impetuous decisions. And despite that Alix found himself drawn once again to the massive window through which he'd seen Leila across the square last night. The shop was in darkness now, the blind pulled firmly down.

A sense of impotent frustration gripped him even more fiercely now. The upstairs was in darkness too. Was she out? With another man? Saying yes to him? Alix tensed all over at that thought and had to relax consciously. He did not *do* jealousy. Not since he'd kicked his naked bodyguard out of his traitorous lover's bed. And had that even been jealousy? Or just young injured male pride?

He emitted a sound of irritation and plucked a phone out of his pocket. He was connected in seconds and said curtly, 'I want you to find out everything you can about a woman called Leila Verughese. She owns a perfume shop on the Place Vendôme in Paris.'

Alix terminated the connection. He told himself that she was most likely playing a game. Hard to get. But he didn't really care—because he was no woman's fool any more and, game or no game, he *would* have her and sate this burning urge before his life changed irrevocably and became one of duty and responsibility.

She didn't have the power to derail him. No woman did.

For two days Leila stood in her shop, acutely aware of Alix Saint Croix's cavalcade sweeping in and out of the square. Every time his sleek car drove past she tensed inwardly—as if waiting for him to stop and get out and come in again. To ask her to dinner again.

She hated it that she knew when his cars were parked outside the hotel. It made her feel jittery, on edge.

Just then her phone rang, and she jumped and cursed softly before answering it. It was the hotel. They wanted Leila to bring over an assortment of perfumes for one of their guests.

She agreed and put the phone down, immediately feeling nervous. Which was ridiculous. This wasn't an unusual request—hotel guests often spotted the shop and asked for a personal service. At one time Leila had gone over with perfumes for a foreign president's wife.

Even though she would be venturing far too near to the lion in his lair, she welcomed the diversion and set about gathering as many diverse samples of perfumes as she could.

On arrival at the hotel, dressed smartly in a dark trouser suit and white shirt, hair up, and with her specially fortified and protective wheelie suitcase, Leila was shown to the top floor by a duty manager.

The same floor as Alix Saint Croix's suite.

She felt a flutter of panic, but pushed it down as the lift doors opened and she stepped into the opulent luxury of one of the hotel's most sumptuous floors.

To her vast relief they were heading in the opposite direction from the suite she'd watched so closely the other night.

The duty manager opened the door to the suite and ushered Leila in, saying, 'Your clients will be here shortly—they said to go ahead and set up while you're waiting.'

Leila smiled. 'Okay, thank you.'

When she was alone she set about opening her case and taking out some bottles, glad to have the distraction of what she did best. No time to think about—

She heard the door open behind her and stood up and turned around with a smile on her face, expecting to see a woman.

The smile promptly slid off her face when she saw Alix Saint Croix and the door closing softly behind him. *Client*, not clients. For a long moment Leila was only aware of her heartbeat, fast and hard. He was dressed in a white shirt and dark trousers. Sleeves rolled up, top button open. Hands in his pockets. He was looking at her with a gleam in his eyes that told her the predator had tracked down his prey.

So why was she suddenly feeling a thrum of excitement?

He took a step further into the room and inclined his head towards her suitcase, which was open on an ottoman. 'Do you supply men's scents also?'

Leila was determined not to appear as ruffled as she felt. She said coolly, 'First of all, I don't appreciate being ambushed, Mr Saint Croix. But, as I'm here now—yes, I do men's scents also.'

Alix Saint Croix looked at her with that enigmatic gaze, a small smile playing around his mouth. 'The hotel told me that you regularly come to do personal consultations. Do you regard *all* clients as ambushing you?'

Leila's face coloured. 'Of course not.' She felt flustered now. 'Look, why don't we get on with it? I'm sure you're a busy man.'

He came closer, rolling his sleeves up further as he said, with a definite glint in his grey eyes, 'On the contrary, I have all the time in the world.'

Leila's hands clenched into fists at her sides. She boiled inside at the way he'd so neatly caught her and longed to be able to storm out…but to where? Back to an empty shop? To polish the endless glass shelves? He'd just suggested a lucrative personal consultation—even if his actions were nefarious. Not to mention the wad of cash he'd left her the other day…

Swallowing her ire, and not liking the way he was getting under her skin so easily, she forced a smile and said, 'Of course. Then, please, sit down.'

Leila was careful to take a chair at a right angle to the couch. Briskly she took out some of her sample bottles containing pure oils and a separate mixer bottle.

As he passed her to sit down she unconsciously found herself searching for his scent again, and it hit her as powerfully as it had the first time. Leila had a sudden and fantastical image of herself having access to this man's naked body and being allowed to spend as much time as she liked discovering the secret scents of his very essence, so that she could try to analyse them and distil them into a perfume.

She cursed her wayward imagination and said, without looking at him, 'Had you any particular scent in mind? What do you usually like?'

She was aware of strong thighs in her peripheral vision, his trousers doing little to hide their length or muscularity.

'I have no idea,' he said dryly. 'I get sent new perfumes all the time and usually just pick whatever appeals to me in the moment. But generally I don't like anything too heavy.'

Leila glanced at him sharply. His face was expressionless, but there was an intensity in his eyes that made her nervous. For a moment she could almost believe he wasn't talking about scents at all, and felt like telling him to save his breath if he was warning her obliquely that he wasn't into commitment—because she had no intention of getting to know him any better.

She couldn't deny, though, how her very body seemed to hum in his presence.

Instinctively she reached for a bottle and pulled it out, undoing the stopper. She sniffed for a moment and then dipped a smelling strip into the bottle and extracted it and held it out towards him. 'What do you think of this, Monsieur Saint Croix?'

'Please…' he purred. 'Call me Alix.'

Leila tensed, her hand held out, refusing to give in to his unashamed flirtation. Eventually, eyes sparkling as he registered her obvious struggle against him, he took the sliver of paper and Leila snatched her hand back.

He kept his eyes on her as he smelled it carefully, passing it over and back under his nose. She saw something flare in his eyes, briefly, and felt an answering rush of heat under her skin.

Consideringly, he said, 'I like it—what is it?'

'It's fougère—a blend of notes based on lavender, oakmoss and coumarin: a derivative of the tonka bean. It's a good base on which to build a scent if you like it.'

He handed her back the tester and lifted a brow. 'The tonka bean?'

Leila nodded as she pulled out another bottle. 'It's a soft, woody note. We extract ingredients for a scent from anything and everything.'

She was beginning to feel more relaxed, concentrating on her work as if there *wasn't* a whole subtext going on between her and this man. Maybe she could just ignore it.

'It was developed in the late eighteen-hundreds by Houbigant and I find it evocative of a woody, ferny environment.'

Leila handed him another smelling strip.

'Try this.'

He took it and looked at her again. She found it hard to take her eyes away as he breathed deep. Every move this man made was so boldly sensual. Sexy. It made Leila want to curl in on herself and try not to be noticed.

'This is more…exotic?'

Leila answered, 'It's oudh—quite rare. From agarwood. A very distinctive scent—people either love it or hate it.'

He looked at her, his mouth quirking slightly. 'I like it. What does that say about me?'

Leila shrugged minutely as she reached for another bottle, trying to affect nothing but professionalism. 'Just that you respond to the more complex make-up of the scent. It's perhaps no surprise that a king should favour such a rare specimen.'

Immediately tension sprang up between them, and Leila busied herself opening another bottle.

Alix Saint Croix's voice was sharper this time. 'A king in exile, to be more accurate. Does that make a difference?'

Leila looked at him as she handed him another sample and said, equally coolly, 'I'm sure it doesn't. You're still a king, after all, are you not?'

He made a dissenting sound as he took the new tester. Leila wondered how much more patience he would have for this game they were playing. As if someone like him *really* had time for a personal perfume consultation…

She looked to see him sniff the strip and saw how he immediately recoiled from the smell. He grimaced, and Leila had to bite back a smile.

'What is *that*?'

She reached across and took the paper back. 'It's extracted from the narcissus flower.'

His mouth curled up slightly. 'Should I take that as a compliment? That I don't immediately resonate with the narcissus?'

Leila avoided looking at him and started packing up her bottles, eager to get away from this man. 'If you like any of those scents we tested I can make something up for you.'

'I'd like that. But I want you to add something I haven't considered…something you think would uniquely suit me.'

Leila tightened inwardly at the prospect of choosing something unique to him. She closed the case and looked at him. 'I'm afraid I will be bound to disappoint you. Perfume is such a personal—'

'And I'd like you to deliver it personally this evening.' He cut her off as if she hadn't even been talking.

Leila stood up abruptly and looked down at him. 'Monsieur Saint Croix, while I appreciate the custom you've given me today, I'm afraid I…'

He stood up then too, and the words dried in her throat as his tall body towered over hers. They were too close.

His voice was low, with a thread of steel. 'Are you seriously telling me that you're turning down the opportunity to custom make a scent for the royal house of Isle Saint Croix?'

When he said it like that Leila could hear her mother's voice in her head, shrill and panicked, *Are you completely crazy?* What was she doing? In her bid to escape from this disturbing tension was she prepared to jeopardise the most potentially lucrative sale she'd had in years? The merest hint of a professional association with a *king*, no less, and her sales would go through the roof.

In a small voice she finally said, 'No, of course I wouldn't turn down such an opportunity. I can put a couple of sample fragrances together and deliver them to the hotel later. You can let me know which you prefer.'

His eyes were a mesmerising shade of pewter. 'One scent, Leila, and I want you to bring it to me personally. Say seven p.m.?'

Her name on his lips felt absurdly intimate, as if he'd just touched her. She glared at him but had no room to manoeuvre. And then she told herself to get a grip. Alix Saint Croix might be disturbing her on all sorts of levels but he was hardly going to kidnap her. *He wouldn't need to.* That was the problem. Leila was afraid that if she had much more contact with him, her defences would start to feel very flimsy.

Hiding her irritation at how easily he was sweeping aside her reservations, she bent down and closed her suitcase—but before she could lift it off the ottoman he brushed her hand aside and took it, wrapped a big hand firmly around the handle.

Leila straightened, face flushed. He extended a hand and lifted a brow. 'After you.'

Much to her embarrassment, he insisted on escorting her all the way down to the lobby and seemed to be oblivious to the way everyone jumped to attention—not least his security guards. He called one of them over and handed the thickset man the case, instructing him to carry it back to the shop for Leila. Her protests fell on deaf ears.

And then, before she could leave, he said, 'What time shall I send Ricardo to escort you to the hotel?'

Leila turned and looked up. She was about to assert that she'd had no problem crossing the square on her own for some two decades, but as soon as she saw the look in his eye she said with a resigned sigh, 'Five to seven.'

He dipped his head. 'Till then, Leila.'

Once back in his own suite, Alix stood looking across the square for a long time. Leila's reluctance to acquiesce to him intrigued him. Anticipation tightened his gut. Even though he knew this was likely just a game on her part, he was prepared to indulge it because he wanted her. And he had time on his hands.

He felt a mild pang of guilt now when he thought of what his security team had reported to him about her.

The Verughese family were wealthy and respectable in India. A long line of perfumers, supplying scents to maharajas and the richest in society. There were a scant few lines about Deepika Verughese, who had been Leila's mother. She'd come to France after breaking off relations with her family, where she'd proceeded to have one daughter: Leila. No mention of a father.

In all other respects she was squeaky clean. No headlines had ever appeared about her.

He felt something vibrate in his pocket and extracted a small, sleek mobile phone. Without checking to see who it was, and not taking his eyes off his quarry across the square, he answered, 'Yes?'

It was his chief advisor, and Alix welcomed the distraction, reminded of the bigger picture.

He turned his back to the view. 'How are the plans for the referendum coming along?'

Isle Saint Croix was due to vote within two weeks on whether or not they wanted Alix to return as King. It was still too volatile for Alix to be in the country himself, so he was depending on loyal politicians and his people, who had campaigned long and hard to restore the monarchy. Finally the end goal was in sight. But it was a very delicate balancing act that could all come tumbling down at any moment.

The ruling party in Isle Saint Croix were ruthless, and only the fact that they'd had to reluctantly agree to let international observers into the country had saved the process from falling apart already.

Andres was excited. 'The polls are showing in your favour, but not so much that it's unduly worrying the military government. They're still arrogant enough to believe they're in control.'

Alix listened to him reiterate what he already knew, but it was still reassuring. Something bittersweet pierced his heart. When he regained the throne he would finally have a chance to avenge his younger brother's brutal death.

Alix tuned back into the conversation when the other man cleared his voice awkwardly and said, 'Is it true that your affair with Carmen Desanto is over? It was in the papers today.'

Alix's mouth tightened. Only because of the fact that Andres was one of his oldest and most trusted friends did he even contemplate answering the question. 'What of it?'

'Well, it's unfortunate timing. The busier you can look with very *un*political concerns the better—to lull the regime on Isle Saint Croix into a false sense of security. Even if they hear rumours of you gaining support from abroad, when they see pictures in the papers...'

He didn't need to finish. Alix would appear to be the louche and unthreatening King in exile he'd always been. Still, he didn't like to be dictated to like this.

'Well,' he said with a steely undertone, 'I'm afraid that,

as convenient a front as Carmen might have proved to be, I wasn't prepared to put up with her inane chatter for any longer.'

An image popped into Alix's head of another woman. Someone whose chatter he wouldn't mind listening to. And he very much doubted that *she* ever chattered inanely. Those beautiful eyes were far too intelligent.

On the other end of the phone Andres sighed theatrically. 'Look, all I'm saying is that now would be a really good time to be living up to your reputation as an eligible bachelor, cutting a swathe through the beauties of the world.'

Alix had only been interested in a very personal conquest before now, but suddenly the thought of pursuing Leila Verughese took on a whole new dimension. It was, in fact, completely justifiable.

A small smile curled his lips. 'Don't worry, Andres. I'm sure I can think of something to keep the media hounds happy.'

When the knock came on Alix's door at about one minute past seven that evening he didn't like to acknowledge the anticipation rushing through his blood. The reminder that Leila was getting to him on a level that was unprecedented was not welcome. He told himself it was just lust. Chemical. Controllable.

He strode forward and opened the door to see Leila with a vaguely mutinous look on her beautiful face and Ricardo behind her. Alix nodded to his bodyguard and the man melted away.

Alix stood back and held the door open. 'Please, come in.'

He noted that Leila hadn't changed outfits since earlier. She was still wearing the smart dark trouser suit and her hair was pulled back into a low, sleek ponytail. She wore not a scrap of make-up, yet her features stood out as if someone had lovingly painted her.

The pale olive skin, straight nose, lush mouth and startling green eyes combined together to such an effect that Alix could only mentally shake his head as he followed her into his suite... How did such a woman as this work quietly in a perfume shop, going largely unnoticed?

She turned to face him in the palatial living room and held up a glossy House of Leila bag. 'Your fragrance, Monsieur Saint Croix.'

Alix bit back the urge to curse and said smoothly, 'Leila, I've asked you to call me Alix.'

Her eyes glittered. 'Well, I don't think it's appropriate. You're a client—'

'A client who,' he inserted smoothly, 'has just paid a significant sum of money for a customised fragrance.'

Her mouth shut and remorse lit her eyes. Alix was fascinated again by the play of unguarded emotions. God knew he certainly hadn't revealed emotion himself for years. And the women he dealt with probably wouldn't know a real emotion if it jumped up and bit them on the ass.

She looked at him and he felt short of breath, acutely aware of the thrust of her perfect breasts against the silk of her shirt.

'Very well. Alix.'

Her mouth and tongue wrapping around his name had an effect similar to that if she'd put her mouth on his body intimately. Blood rushed south and he hardened.

Gritting his jaw against the onset of a fierce arousal that made a mockery of any illusion of control, Alix responded, 'That wasn't so hard, was it?' He groaned inwardly at his unfortunate choice of words and reached for the bag she still held out in a bid to distract her from seeing her seismic effect in his body.

With the bag in his hand he gestured for her to sit down. 'Please, make yourself comfortable. Would you like a drink?'

Leila's hands twisted in front of her. 'No, thank you. I really should be getting back—'

'Don't you want to know if I like the scent or not?'

Her mouth stayed open and eventually she said, 'Of course I do... But you could send word if you don't like it.'

Alix frowned minutely and moved closer to Leila, cocking his head to one side. 'Why are you so nervous with me?'

She swallowed. He could see the long slim column of her throat, the pulse beating near the base. Hectic.

'I'm not nervous.'

He came closer and a warm seeping of colour made her skin flush.

'Liar. You're ready to jump out of that window to get away from me right now.'

One graceful brow arched. 'Not a reaction you're used to?'

Alix's mouth quirked. The tension was diffused a little. 'No, not usually.'

He indicated again for Leila to sit down and after a moment, when he really wasn't sure if she'd just walk out, she moved over to the couch and sat down. Something relaxed inside him.

He put down the bag containing the scent while he poured himself a drink and glanced at her over his shoulder. 'Are you sure I can't get you anything?'

She'd been taking in the room, eyes wide, and suddenly all its opulence felt garish to Alix.

Those eyes clashed with his. 'Okay,' she said huskily. 'I'll have a little of whatever you're having.'

It was crazy. Alix wanted to howl in triumph at this concession. At the fact that she was still here, when usually he was batting women away.

'Bourbon?'

She half nodded and shrugged. 'I've never tried it before.'

There was something incredibly disarming about her easy admission. Like watching the play of emotion on her face and in her eyes. Alix brought the drinks over and was careful to take a seat at right angles to the couch, knowing for certain that she'd bolt if he sat near her.

He handed her the glass and she took it. He held his out. '*Santé*, Leila.'

She tipped her glass towards his and took a careful sip, as he took a sip of his own. He watched her reaction, saw her eyes watering slightly, her cheeks warming again. His own drink slipped down his throat, making his already warm body even hotter.

'What do you think?'

She considered for a moment and then gave a tiny smile. 'It's like fire... I like it.'

'Yes,' Alix said faintly, transfixed by Leila's mouth, 'It's like fire.'

A moment stretched between them, and then she dropped her gaze from his and put her glass down on the table to indicate the bag she'd brought. 'You should see if you like the scent.'

Alix put down his own glass and took the bag, extracting a gold box embossed with a black line around the edges. It had a panel on the front with a label that said simply *Alix Saint Croix*.

Alix opened the box and took out the heavy and beautifully cut glass bottle, with its black lid and distinctive gold piping. It was masculine—solid.

'It's quite strong,' Leila said, as he took off the lid and looked at her. 'You only need a small amount. Try it on the back of your hand.'

Alix sprayed and then bent his head. He wasn't ready for the immediate effect on his senses. It impacted deep down in his gut—so many layers of scent, filtering through his brain and throwing up images like a slide-show going too fast for him to analyse.

He was thrown back in time to his home on the island, with the sharp, tangy smell of the sea in the air, and yet he could smell the earth too, and the scent of the exotic flowers that bloomed on Isle Saint Croix. He could even smell something oriental, spicy, that made him think of his Moorish ancestors who had given the island its distinctive architecture.

He wasn't prepared for the sharp pang of emotion that gripped him as a memory surged: him and his younger brother, playing, carefree, near the sea.

'What's in it?' he managed to get out.

Leila was looking concerned. 'You don't like it?'

'Like' was too flimsy a word for what this scent was doing to him. Alix stood up abruptly, feeling acutely exposed. *Dieu.* Was she a witch? He strode over to the window and kept his back to her, brought his hand up to smell again.

The initial shock of the impact was lessening as the scent opened out and mellowed. It was *him*. The scent was everything that was deep inside him, where no one could see his true self. Yet this woman had got it—after only a couple of meetings and a few hours.

CHAPTER THREE

LEILA STOOD UP, not sure how to respond. She'd never seen someone react so forcefully to a scent before.

'I researched a little about the island, to find out what its native flowers were, and I approximated them as closely as I could with what I have available in the shop. And I added citrus and calone, which has always reminded me of a sea breeze.'

Alix Saint Croix looked huge, formidable, against the window and the autumnal darkness outside. Her first reaction when she'd met this man had been fascination, a feeling of being dazzled, and since then her instinct had been to run away—fast. But now her feet were glued to the floor.

'If you don't like it—'

'I like it.'

His response was short, sharp. He sounded almost... *angry*. Leila was completely confused.

Hesitantly she said, 'Are you sure? You don't sound very pleased.'

He turned around then and thrust both hands into his pockets. His chest was broad, the darkness of his skin visible under his shirt. He looked at her closely and shook his head, as if trying to clear it.

Finally he said, 'I'm just a little surprised. The fragrance is not what I was expecting.'

Leila shrugged. 'A customised scent has a bigger impact than a generic designer scent...'

His mouth quirked sexily and he came back over to the couch. Leila couldn't take her eyes off him.

'It certainly has an impact.'

'If it's too strong I can—'

'No.' Alix's voice cut her off. 'I don't want you to change it.'

A knock came on the door then, and Leila flinched a little. She was so caught up in this man's reaction and his charisma that she'd almost forgotten where she was. The seductive warmth of the bourbon in her belly didn't help.

Alix said, 'That's dinner. I took the liberty of ordering for two, if you'd care to join me?'

Leila just looked at him and felt again that urge to run—but also a stronger urge to stay. *Rebel.* Even though she wasn't exactly sure who she was rebelling against. Herself and every instinct screaming at her to run? Or the ghost of her mother's disappointment?

She justified her weakness to herself: this man had thrown more business her way than she'd see in the next month. She should be polite. *Ha!* said a snide inner voice. *There's nothing polite about the way you feel around him.*

She ignored that and said, as coolly as she could, 'Only if it's not too much of an imposition.'

He had a very definite mocking glint to his eye. 'It's no imposition...really.'

Alix went to the door and opened it to reveal obsequious staff who proceeded straight towards a room off the main reception area. Within minutes they were leaving again, and Alix was waiting for Leila to precede him into the dining room—which was as sumptuously decorated as the rest of the suite.

She caught a glimpse of a bedroom through an open

door and almost tripped over her feet to avoid looking that way again. It brought to mind too easily the way that woman had stripped so nonchalantly for her lover. And how Alix had maintained that nothing had happened in spite of appearances.

Why should she even care, when he was probably lying?

Leila almost balked at that point, but as if sensing her trepidation, Alix pulled out a chair and looked at her pointedly. No escape. She moved forward and sat down, looking at the array of food laid out on the table. There was enough for a small army.

Alix must have seen something on her face, because he grimaced a little and said, 'I wasn't sure if you were vegetarian or not, so I ordered a selection.'

Leila couldn't help a wry smile. 'I *am* vegetarian, actually—mostly my mother's influence. Though I do sometimes eat fish.'

Alix started to put some food on a plate for her: a mixture of tapas-type starters, including what looked like balls of rice infused with herbs and spices. The smells had her mouth watering, and she realised that she hadn't eaten since earlier that day, her stomach having been too much in knots after seeing Alix Saint Croix again, and then thinking about him all afternoon as she'd worked on his fragrance.

She could smell it now, faintly—exotic and spicy, with that tantalising hint of citrus—and her insides quivered. It suited him: light, but with much darker undertones.

He handed her the plate and then plucked a chilled bottle of white wine out of an ice bucket. Leila wasn't used to drinking, and could still feel the effects of the bourbon, so she held up a hand when Alix went to pour her some wine.

'I'll stick to water, thanks.'

As he poured himself some wine he asked casually, 'Where are your parents from?'

Leila tensed inevitably as the tall, shadowy and indistinct shape of her father came into her mind's eye. She'd only ever seen him in photos in the newspaper. Tightly she answered, 'My mother was a single parent. She was from India.'

'Was?'

Leila nodded and concentrated on spearing some food with her fork. 'She died a few years ago.'

'I'm sorry. That must have been hard if it was just the two of you.'

Leila was a little taken aback at the sincerity she heard in his voice and said quietly, 'It was the hardest thing.'

She avoided his eyes and put a forkful of food in her mouth, not expecting the explosion of flavours from the spice-infused rice ball. She looked at him and he smiled at her reaction, chewing his own food.

When he could speak he said, 'My personal chef is here. He's from Isle Saint Croix, so he sticks to the local cuisine. It's a mixture of North African and Mediterranean.'

Relieved to be moving away from personal areas, Leila said, 'I've never tasted anything like it.' Then she admitted ruefully, 'I haven't travelled much, though.'

'You were born here?'

Leila reached for her water, as much to cool herself down as anything else. 'Yes, my mother travelled over when she was pregnant. My father was French.'

'Was?'

Leila immediately regretted letting that slip out. But her mother was no longer alive. Surely the secret didn't have to be such a secret any more? But then she thought of how easily her father had turned his back on them and repeated her mother's words, used whenever anyone had asked a similar question. 'He died a long time ago. I never knew him.'

To her relief, Alix didn't say anything to that, just looked at her consideringly. They ate in companionable silence for a few minutes, and Leila tried not to think too hard about where she was and who she was with.

When she'd cleared half her plate she sneaked a look at Alix. He was sitting back, cradling his glass of wine, looking at her. And just like that her skin prickled with heat.

'I hope I didn't lose you too much custom by taking up your attention today?'

He looked entirely unrepentant, and in spite of herself Leila had to allow herself a small wry smile. 'No—the opposite. The business has been struggling to get back on track since the recession...niche industries like mine were the worst hit.'

Alix frowned. 'Yet you kept hold of your shop?'

Leila nodded, tensing a little at the thought of the uphill battle to restore sales. 'I've owned it outright since my mother died.'

'That's good—but you *could* sell. You don't need me to tell you what that shop and flat must be worth in this part of Paris.'

Leila's insides clenched hard. 'I won't *ever* sell,' she said in a low voice. The shop and the flat were her mother's legacy to her—a safe haven. Security. She barely knew this man...she wasn't about to confide in him.

Feeling self-conscious again, she took her napkin from her lap and put it on the table. That silver gaze narrowed on her.

'I should go. Thank you for dinner—you really didn't have to.'

She saw a muscle twitch in Alix's jaw and half expected—*wanted?*—him to stop her from going.

But he just stood up smoothly and said, 'Thank you for joining me.'

Much to Leila's sense of disorientation, Alix made no effort to detain her with offers of tea or coffee. He picked up the bag that she'd had with her when she'd arrived and handed it to her in the main reception room.

Feeling at a loss, and not liking the sense of disappointment that he was letting her go so easily, Leila said again, 'Thank you.'

Alix bowed slightly towards her and once again she was struck by his sheer beauty and all that potent masculinity. He looked as if he was about to speak some platitude, then he stopped and said, 'Actually... I have tickets to the opera for tomorrow evening. I wonder if you'd like to join me?'

Leila didn't trust his all-too-innocent façade for a second—as if he'd just thought of it. But she couldn't think straight because giddy relief was mocking her for the disappointment she'd felt just seconds ago because he was letting her go so easily.

She was dealing with a master here.

This was not the first time a man had asked her out but it still hit her in the solar plexus like a blow. Her last disastrous dating experience rose like a dark spectre in her memory—except this man in front of her eclipsed Pierre Gascon a hundred times over. Enough to give her a little frisson of satisfaction.

As if *any* man could compete with this tall, dark specimen before her. *Sexy.* Leila had never been overtly aware of sexual longing before. But now she was—she could feel the awareness throbbing in her blood, between her legs.

And it was that awareness of how out of her depth Alix Saint Croix made her feel that had Leila blurting out, 'I really don't think it would be a good idea.' *Coward*, whispered a voice.

He lifted a brow in lazy enquiry. 'And why would that be? You're single...I'm single. We're two consenting adults. I'm offering a pleasant way to spend the evening. That's all.'

Now she felt gauche. She was thinking of sex when he certainly wasn't. 'I'm just...not exactly in your league, Monsieur Saint Croix—'

'It's Alix,' he growled, coming closer. 'Call me Alix.'

Leila swallowed, caught in the beam of those incredible eyes. 'Alix...'

'That's better. Now, tell me again exactly why this is not a good idea?'

Feeling cornered and angry now—with herself as much as him—Leila flung out a hand. 'I own a shop and you're a king. We're not exactly on a level footing.'

Alix cocked his head to one side. 'You're a perfumer, are you not? A very commendable career.'

Unable to keep the bitterness out of her voice, Leila said, 'To be a perfumer one needs to be making perfumes.'

'Something I've no doubt you'll do when your business recovers its equilibrium.'

His quiet and yet firm encouragement made something glow in Leila's chest. She ruthlessly pushed it down. This man could charm the devil over to the light side.

'Don't you have more important things to be doing?'

A curious expression she couldn't decipher crossed his hard-boned face before his mouth twitched and he said, 'Not right now, no.'

Leila's stubborn refusal to accede to his wishes was having a bizarre effect on Alix. He could quite happily stay here for hours and spar with her, watching those expressions cross her face and her gorgeous eyes spark and glow.

'Don't you know,' he said carefully, watching her reaction with interest, 'that feigning uninterest is one sure way to get a man interested in you?'

Immediately her cheeks were suffused with colour and her back went poker straight with indignation. Eyes glittering, she said, 'I am *not* feigning uninterest, Mr Saint Croix, I am genuinely mystified as to why you are persisting like this—and to be perfectly frank I think I'd prefer it if you just left me alone.'

He took a step closer. 'Really, Leila? I could let you walk out of this suite right now and you'll never see me again.' He waited a beat and then said softly, 'If that's *really* what you want. But I don't think it is.'

Oh, God. He'd seen her disappointment. She'd never been any good at hiding her emotions. She'd also never felt so hot with the need to break out of some confinement holding her back.

She hadn't felt this hungry urgency with Pierre. He'd been far more subtle—and ultimately manipulative. Alix was direct. And there was something absurdly comforting about that. There were no games. He wasn't dressing his words up with illusions of more being involved. It made her breathless.

Her extended silence had made something go hard in Alix's eyes and Leila felt a dart of panic go through her. She sensed that he would stop pursuing her if she asked him to. If he did indeed believe she was stringing him along. Which she wasn't. Or was she? Unconsciously?

She hated to think that she might be capable of such a thing, but she couldn't deny the thrilling rush of something illicit every time she saw him. The rush of sparring with him. The rush each time he came back even though she'd said no.

Leila felt as if she was skirting around the edges of a

very large and angry fire that mesmerised her as much as it made her fear its heat. She'd shut down after her experience with Pierre, dismayed at coming to terms with the fact that she'd made such a huge misjudgement. But now she could feel a part of her expanding inside again, demanding to be heard. To be set free. Another chance.

She'd never been to the opera. Pierre's most exciting invitation had been to a trip down the Seine, which Leila had done a million times with her mother. The sense of yearning got stronger.

She heard herself asking, 'It's *just* a trip to the opera?'

The hardness in Alix's eyes softened, but he was careful enough not to show that he'd gained a point.

'Yes, Leila, it's just a simple trip to the opera. If you can close a little early tomorrow I'll pick you up at five.'

Closing a little early would hardly damage her already dented business. She took a deep breath and tried not to let this moment feel bigger than it should. 'Very well. I'll accept your invitation.'

Alix took up her hand and raised it to his mouth before brushing a very light, almost imperceptible kiss across the back of it. Even so, his breath burned her skin.

'I look forward to it, Leila. *A bientôt.*'

At about three o'clock the next day Leila found herself dealing with an unusual flurry of customers, and it took her a couple of seconds to notice the thickset man waiting just inside the door. When she finally registered that it was Ricardo, Alix's bodyguard, she noticed that he had a big white box in his hands.

She went over and he handed it to her, saying gruffly, 'A gift from Mr Saint Croix.'

Leila took the box warily and glanced at her customers, who were all engrossed in trying out the samples she'd been showing them. She looked back to Ricardo and felt a trickle of foreboding. 'Can you wait for a second?'

He nodded, and if Leila had had the time to appreciate how out of place he looked against the backdrop of delicate perfume bottles she might have smiled.

She suspected that she knew what was in the box.

She ducked into a small anteroom behind the counter and opened it to reveal layers of expensive-looking silver tissue paper. Underneath the paper she saw a glimmer of silk, and gasped as she pulled out the most beautiful dress she'd ever seen.

It was a very light green, with one simple shoulder strap and a ruched bodice. The skirt fell to the floor from under the bust in layers of delicate chiffon. On further investigation Leila saw that there were matching shoes and even underwear. Her face burned at that. It burned even more when she realised that Alix had got her size spot-on.

She felt tempted to march right across the square and tell him to shove his date, but she held on to her temper. This was how he must operate with *all* his women. And he was arrogant enough to think that Leila was just like them?

'What do you mean, she wouldn't accept it?'

Ricardo looked exceedingly uncomfortable and shifted from foot to foot, before saying *sotto voce*, mindful of the other men in the room, 'She left a note inside the box.'

'Did she now?' Alix curbed his irritation and said curtly, 'Thank you, Ricardo, that will be all.'

Alix had been holding a meeting in his suite, and the other men around the table started to move a little, clearly anticipating a break from the customarily intense sessions Alix conducted. He dismissed them too, with a look that changed their expressions of relief to ones of meek servitude.

When they were all gone Alix flicked open the lid of the box and saw the plain piece of white paper lying on the silver paper with its succinct message:

Thank you, but I can dress myself.
Leila.

Alix couldn't help his mouth quirking in a smile. Had any woman ever handed him back a gift? Not in his memory.

He let the lid drop down and stood up to walk over to the window of his suite, which looked out over the square below.

For a large portion of his life, ever since his dramatic escape from Isle Saint Croix all those years ago, he'd felt like a caged animal—forced into this role of pretending that he *wasn't* engaged in an all-out battle to regain his throne. The prospect of being on his island again, with the salty tang of the sea in the hot air... Sometimes the yearning for home was almost unbearable.

Alix sighed and let his gaze narrow on the small shop that glinted across the square in the late-afternoon sunlight. He could see the familiar slim white-coated shape moving back and forth. The caged animal within him got even more restless. The yearning was replaced with sharp anticipation.

It would be no hardship to pursue Miss Verughese and let the world think nothing untoward was going on behind the scenes. No hardship at all.

Leila looked at herself in the mirror and had a sudden attack of nerves. Maybe she'd been really stupid to send Alix's gift back to him? She'd never been to the opera—she wasn't even sure what the dress code was, except posh.

The scent she'd put on so sparingly drifted up, and for a moment she wanted to run and wash it off. It wasn't her usual scent, which was light and floral. This was a scent that had always fascinated her: one of her mother's most sensual creations. It had called to Leila from the shelf just after she'd locked up before coming upstairs to get ready.

It was called *Dark Desiring*. Her mother had had a penchant for giving their perfumes enigmatic names. As soon as Leila had sprayed a little on her wrist she'd heard her mother's voice in her head: *'This scent is for a woman, Leila. The kind of woman who knows what she wants and gets it. You will be that woman someday, and you won't be foolish like your mother.'*

She felt the scent now, deep in the pit of her belly. Felt its dark sensuality, earthy musky notes and exotic floral arrangement. It was so unlike her…and yet it resonated with her. But she felt exposed wearing it—as if it would be obvious to everyone that she was trying to be something she wasn't.

The doorbell sounded… Too late to remove it now, even if she wanted to.

She made her way downstairs, her heart palpitating in her chest. She thrust aside memories of another man she'd let too close. It had been as if as soon as her mother's influence had been removed Leila had automatically sought out proof that not all men weren't to be trusted. But that had spectacularly backfired and proved her *very* wrong.

Walking through the darkened shop, Leila forced the clamouring memories down. She'd learnt her lesson. She was no fool any more. She still wanted something different from her mother's experience, but Alix Saint Croix was the last man to offer such a thing. So, if anything, she couldn't be safer than with this man.

She sucked in a big breath and opened the door. The sky was dusky outside and Alix blocked most of it with his broad shoulders. He was dressed in a classic black tuxedo and white bow tie under his overcoat. Leila's mouth went dry. That assurance of safety suddenly felt very flimsy.

She wasn't even aware that Alix's eyes had widened on her when she'd appeared.

'You look beautiful.'

She stopped gawking at him long enough to meet his eyes. And those nerves gripped her again as she gestured shyly to her outfit. 'I wasn't sure... I hope it's appropriate?'

Alix lifted his eyes to hers. 'It's stunning. You look like a princess.'

Leila blushed and busied herself pulling the door behind her and locking it to deflect his scrutiny.

The outfit was a traditional Indian *salwar kameez* with a bit of a modern twist. The tunic was made out of green and gold silk, with slim-fitting trousers in the same shade of green. She had on gold strappy sandals that she'd bought one day on a whim but never worn. A loose chiffon throw was draped over her shoulders and she'd put her hair up in a high bun. She wore ornate earrings that had belonged to her mother—like a talisman that might protect her from falling into the vortex that this man created whenever he was near.

The driver of the sleek car parked nearby was holding the door open, and Leila slid into the luxurious confines as Alix joined her from the other side. She plucked nervously at the material of her tunic as they pulled away.

Alix took her hand and she looked at him.

'You look amazing. No other woman will be dressed the same.'

Leila quirked a wry smile, liking the feel of Alix's

hand around hers far too much. 'That's what I'm suddenly afraid of.'

He shook his head. 'You'll stand out like a bird of paradise—they'll be insanely jealous.'

Leila gave a small dissenting sound and went to pull her hand back, but Alix gripped it tighter and lifted it up, turning her wrist. He frowned slightly and bent to smell. Leila's heart thumped, hard.

He looked at her. 'This isn't your usual scent?'

Damn him for noticing. Leila cursed her impetuosity and felt as if that scarlet letter was on her forehead for all to see. She pulled her hand back. 'No, it's a different scent—one more suitable for evenings.'

'I like it.'

Leila could smell his scent too. The one she'd made him. She knew that it lingered on his skin from when he'd put it on much earlier that day—it didn't have the sharp tang of having been recently applied. She thought of their scents now, mingling and wrapping around one another. It made her feel unbearably aware of the fact that they were so close. Aware of the warm blood pumping just under their skin, making those scents mellow and change subtly.

It was an alchemy that happened to everyone in a totally different way, as the perfume responded uniquely to each individual.

She finally looked away from Alix to see that they were leaving the confines of the city and heading towards the grittier outskirts. Nowhere near the Paris opera house.

She frowned and looked back at him. 'I thought we were going to the opera?'

'We are.'

'But we're leaving Paris.'

Alix smiled. 'I said we were going to the opera. I didn't say where.'

Flutters of panic made her tense. 'I don't appreciate surprises. Tell me where we're going, please.'

His eyes narrowed on her and Leila bit back the urge to lambast him for assuming she was just some wittering dolly bird, only too happy to let him whisk her off to some unknown location.

Alix's voice had an edge of steel to it when he said, 'We're going to Venice.'

'*Venice?*' Leila squeaked. 'But I don't have my passport. I mean, how can we just—?'

Alix took her hand again and spoke as if he was soothing a nervous horse. 'You don't need your passport. I have diplomatic immunity and you're with me. The flight will take an hour and forty minutes. I'll have you back in Paris and home by midnight. I promise.'

Leila reeled. 'You said flight?'

Alix nodded warily, as if expecting another explosion.

'I've never been on a plane before,' she admitted somewhat warily. As if Alix might be so disgusted with her lack of sophistication that he'd turn around and deliver her home right now.

He just frowned slightly. 'But…how is that possible?'

Leila shrugged, finding to her consternation that once again she was loath to take her hand out of Alix's much bigger one. 'My mother and I…we didn't travel much. Apart from to other parts of France. We went to England once, to visit a factory outside London, but we took the train. My mother was terrified of flying.'

'Well, then,' said Alix throatily, 'do you want to go home? Or do you want to take your first flight? We can turn around right now if you want.'

That was like asking if she wanted to keep moving forward in life or backwards. Leila felt that fire reaching out to lick at her with a tantalising flash of heat. Alix's thumb was rubbing the underside of her wrist, making the flash of heat more intense. Leila thought of the car turning around, of returning to that square and her shop. She felt nauseous.

She shook her head. 'I'd like to fly with you.'

Alix brought her hand to his mouth and kissed it lightly before saying, 'Then let's fly.'

Leila might not be half as sophisticated as his usual women, but even she knew that they were talking about something else entirely—just as the flames of that fire reached out to consume her completely and Alix moved close enough to slant his hard sensual mouth over hers.

She'd been kissed before—by Pierre. But his kiss had been insistent and invasive. Too wet, with no finesse. This was...

Leila lost any sense of being able to string a rational thought together when her mouth opened of its own volition under Alix's and she felt the first electrifying contact of his tongue to hers. She was lost.

CHAPTER FOUR

THE ONLY THING stopping Alix exploding into orbit at the feel of Leila's lush soft mouth under his and the shy touch of her tongue was the hand he'd clamped around her waist. He was rock-hard almost instantaneously. He'd never tasted such sweetness. Her mouth trembled under his and he had to use extreme restraint to go slowly, coaxing her to open up to him.

He felt the hitch in her breathing as their kiss deepened and he gathered her closer to feel the swell of her breasts against his chest. Right at that moment Alix couldn't have remembered his own name. He was drowning in heat and lust and an urgent desire to haul Leila over his lap, so that he could seat her against where he ached most.

She pulled back suddenly and he cracked open his eyes to look down into wide green ones. Leila had her hands on his chest and was pushing at him.

'Please—don't do that again.'

Alix was on unsure ground. Another first. He wasn't used to women pushing him away. And he knew Leila had been enjoying it. She'd been melting into him like his hottest teenage fantasy, and he felt about as suave as a teenager right then. All raging hormones and no control.

Drawing on what little control he *did* still have, Alix moved back, putting space between them. He looked at her. Cheeks flushed, chest rising and falling rapidly, eyes avoiding his. Mouth pink and wet. It made him think of other parts of her that might be wet. He cursed himself silently. Where was his finesse?

He reached out and cupped her jaw, seeing how she tensed. He tipped her chin up so that she had no choice but to look at him. Her eyes were huge and wary. There was an edge of something in her eyes that he couldn't read. He felt a spike of recrimination. Had he been too forceful? But he knew he hadn't. It had nearly killed him to rein himself in.

'Did you have a bad experience with a previous lover?'

She pulled his hand down. 'That's none of your business.'

She avoided his eyes again and he wanted to growl his frustration. But they were pulling into the small private airport now, and staff were rushing to meet the car.

Alix got out and pulled his coat around his body, not liking that he had to conceal his arousal. He glared at the driver who was about to help Leila out of the car and the man ducked back to let Alix take her hand. When she stood up beside him, the breeze blowing a loose tendril of dark hair across one cheek, he had to forcibly stop himself from kissing her again.

Gripping her hand, when he usually avoided public displays of affection like the plague, he led her over to the waiting plane: a small sleek private jet that he used for short hops around Europe. He realised then how much he took things like this for granted. Leila had never even flown before.

He stopped and turned to her. 'You're not frightened, are you?'

She glanced from the plane to him and admitted warily, 'It looks a bit small.'

He grinned and felt the dense band of cynicism around his heart loosen a little. 'It's as safe as houses—I promise.'

He urged her forward and up the steps, past a steward in uniform. He chose two seats opposite each other so he could see Leila's expression. He buckled them both in, and then the plane was taxiing down the runway. With a roar of the throttle, it lifted up into the darkening Paris sky. Alix had had a discreet word with the pilot, and watched Leila's face for her reaction as they climbed into the air.

Her hands were gripping the seat's armrests, and when she cast him a quick glance he raised a brow while shrugging off his overcoat. 'Okay?'

She smiled and it was a bit wobbly. 'I think so.' She put a hand to her belly as if to calm it.

Alix was charmed by her reaction. Her expression was avid as the ground was left behind, and her hands gradually relaxed as the plane rose and gained altitude and then found its cruising level. And then her face became suffused with wonder as she took in the fact that they were flying directly over the city of Paris.

It was perfect timing, with all the lights coming on. Alix looked down through his own window and saw the Eiffel Tower flashing. He'd taken this for granted for so long it was a novelty to see it through someone else's eyes.

Leila felt as if she was in a dream. Her stomach had been churning slightly with the motion of the plane, but it was calming now. To be so high above the city and all its glittering lights…the sheer beauty of it almost moved her to tears. And it was distracting enough to help her block out how amazing that kiss had been. How hard it had been to pull away.

What had finally made her come to her senses had been the realisation that she was being kissed by an expert—who'd kissed scores of far more beautiful women than her.

'Why did your mother hate flying so much?'

Leila composed herself before she looked at Alix, where he was lounging in the chair opposite, long legs stretched out and crossed at the ankle, effectively caging her in. Despite her best efforts, one look at his hard, sensual mouth was bringing their kiss back in glorious Technicolor...the way it had burnt her up.

She forced her gaze up to his eyes and tried to remember his question. 'My mother flew only once in her life, when she came to France from India. It was a traumatic journey for her... She was in disgrace, pregnant and unwed, and was suffering badly from morning sickness.' Leila shrugged lightly, knowing she was leaving so much out of that explanation. 'She always associated flying with that trauma and never wanted to get on a plane again.'

'Aren't you curious about your Indian roots and family?'

An innocuous enough question, but one that had a familiar resentment rising up within Leila. Her mother's family had all but left her for dead—they'd never once contacted her or Leila. Not even when a newspaper had reported that some of them were in Paris for a massive perfume fair.

Leila hid her true emotions under a bland mask. She forced a smile. 'I'm afraid my mother's family cut all ties with us... But perhaps one day I'll go back and visit the country of my ancestors.'

She took refuge in looking at the view again, hoping that Alix wouldn't ask any more personal questions. The lights of the city were becoming sparser. They must be flying further away from Paris now.

But it was as if Alix could read her mind and was deliberately thwarting her. He asked softly, 'Why did you pull back when I kissed you, Leila? I know it wasn't because you really wanted me to stop.'

She froze. She hadn't expected Alix to notice that fleeting moment when she'd felt so insecure. She hadn't wanted it to stop at all…she'd never felt such exquisite pleasure. And the thought of him kissing her again—she knew she wouldn't be able to pull back the next time.

An urgent self-protective need rose up inside her. She had to try and repel Alix on some level—surely a man of a blue-blooded royal line wouldn't want anything to do with the illegitimate daughter of a disgraced Indian woman?

She looked at him, and he was regarding her from under hooded lids.

'You asked before if I'd had a bad experience with a lover…'

Alix sat up straighter. 'You told me it was none of my business.'

'And it's not,' Leila reiterated. 'But, yes, I had a negative encounter with someone, and I don't really wish to repeat the experience.'

Alix went very still, and Leila could see the innate male pride in his expression. He couldn't believe that she would compare him to another man.

'I'm sorry you had to experience that, but you can't damn all men because of one.'

Leila took a breath. Alix wasn't being dissuaded. In spite of the flutters in her belly she went on. 'In fact, if you must know, my mother was rather overprotective.' The flutters increased under Alix's steady regard. 'The truth is that I'm not as experienced as you might—'

'Are you ready for supper, Your Majesty?'

They both looked to see the steward holding out some menus. Relief flooded Leila that she'd been cut off from revealing the ignominious truth of just how inexperienced she was. She welcomed the diversion of taking the menu being proffered.

She imagined that Alix would believe she was still a virgin as much as he'd believe in unicorns. But thankfully, when they were alone again, he didn't seem inclined to continue the discussion.

When she glanced at him, he just sent her an enigmatic glance and said, 'I recommend the risotto—it's vegetarian.'

Leila smiled. 'That sounds good.'

When the young man came back, moments later, Alix ordered. Then he poured them both some champagne. When the flutes were filled and a table had been set between them, Alix lifted his glass and said, with a very definite glint in his eye, 'To new experiences, Leila.'

She cringed inwardly. He didn't have to pursue the discussion. He'd guessed her secret. She lifted her glass too, but said nothing. She got the distinct impression that he still wasn't put off. And, as much as she'd like to tell Alix that flying in a plane was the *only* new experience she was interested in sharing with him, she couldn't formulate the words. Traitorously.

'Why is everyone looking at us?'

Alix looked at Leila incredulously. She had no idea what a sensation she was causing—*had* caused as soon as they'd stepped from his boat and into the ancient *palazzo* on the Grand Canal where the opera was being staged. Leila stood out effortlessly—like a jewel amongst much duller stones. Now it was the interval, and they were seated in a private area to the right of the stage. Private, yet visible.

His mouth quirked. 'They're not looking at us—they're looking at *you*.'

She looked at him and blushed. 'Oh…it's the clothes, isn't it? I should have—'

Alix shook his head, cutting her off. 'It's not the clothes…well, it *is*. But that's because you are more beautiful than any other woman here and you're putting them to shame with your sense of style. Every woman is looking at you and wondering why their finger is not on the pulse.'

Leila's blush deepened, and it had a direct effect on Alix's arousal levels.

'I'm sure that's not it at all. I've never seen so many beautiful people in one place in my entire life. I've never seen anywhere so breathtaking—the canal, this *palazzo*…' She ducked her head for a moment before looking back at him. 'Thank you…this evening has been magical.'

Alix had to school his features. He couldn't remember the last time a woman had thanked him for taking her out.

'You're glad you overcame your reluctance to spend time with me?' he queried innocently.

Her green gaze held his and Alix felt breathless for a second. *Crazy.* Women didn't make him breathless.

Her mouth twitched minutely. 'Yes, I'm glad—but don't let it go to your head.'

An unfortunate choice of words when it made him aware of the part of his anatomy that refused to obey his efforts to control it.

Leila looked so incandescent in that moment—a small smile playing around her mouth, eyes sparkling—that Alix had to curl his hands into fists to stop himself from kissing her again.

The lights dimmed and the cast resumed their places. Alix tore his gaze from her, questioning his sanity and praying that he'd have enough control not to ravish her like a wild animal in the darkened surroundings.

* * *

After the opera had finished Alix took Leila out of the *palazzo* and along the Grand Canal in his boat, to a small rustic Italian restaurant where he was greeted like an old friend by the owner. They ate a selection of small starters and drank wine, and to Leila's surprise the conversation flowed as easily as if they'd known each other for months, not days.

Something had happened—either as soon as she'd agreed to this date or on the plane, when events had become a dizzying spectacle. Or maybe it had been when she'd chosen a different perfume for herself...

She'd stepped over a line—irrevocably. She felt as if she was a different person, inhabiting the same skin. As if she'd thrown off some kind of shackle holding her to the past. She was a little drunk. She knew that. But she'd never felt so light, so...effervescent. So open to new possibilities, experiences.

She wasn't naive enough to think that it would be anything more than transient. Especially with a man like Alix. And that was okay. If anything it was a form of protection. He was practically emblazoned with *Warning!* And *Hazardous!* signs.

She must have giggled a little, because Alix said dryly, 'Something I said was funny?'

Leila shook her head and looked at him, all of a sudden stone-cold sober again. He was beautiful. Their mingled scents wrapped around her. Leila imagined them curling around her brain's synapses, rendering them weak. Making her want what he was offering with those slate-grey eyes—hot with a decadent promise she could only imagine.

Leila realised with a sense of desperation that she *wanted* whatever he was offering. She wanted to lose herself and be broken apart. She wanted to know what it was like. She wanted to taste the forbidden.

She didn't want to go back to her small poky apartment above her failing shop and be the same person. Looking at life passing by across the square. She wanted life to be happening *to her*. She'd never felt it this strongly before. It was his persistent seduction, the perfume, the wine, the opera…leaving her country for the first time. It was his kiss. It was *him*.

Impetuously she leaned forward. 'Do we have to go back to Paris tonight?'

Immediately his gaze narrowed on her. She was acutely conscious of the fact that his jacket and bow tie were gone and his shirt was open at the throat, revealing the strong bronzed column of his neck.

'What are you suggesting?'

Feeling bold for the first time in her life, Leila said, 'I'm suggesting…not going back to Paris. Staying here… in Venice.'

'For the night?'

She nodded. The enormity of what she was doing was dizzying, but she couldn't turn back now. Her heart was thumping.

Alix cocked his head slightly. 'I think you might be a little drunk, Miss Verughese.'

'Perhaps,' she agreed huskily. 'But I know what I'm saying.'

'Do you now…?' Alix looked at her consideringly.

For a second something cold touched Leila's spine. Maybe she had this all wrong. Maybe Alix was just toying with this gauche girl from a shop until a more suitable woman came along? No doubt he was getting a kick out of her untutored reactions to flying and seeing the opera. And now this… Maybe the thought of bedding a virgin wasn't palatable to a man of his undoubted experience and sophisticated tastes? She thought of how that woman had undressed in front of him and her insides contracted painfully. She could never do that.

She looked away, searching for her bag and wrap. 'Forget I said anything. I'm sure you have meetings—'

Suddenly her hand was clasped in his and reluctantly she looked at him. He was intense.

'Are you saying you want to stay in Venice for the night to share my bed, Leila?'

She hated it that he was making her spell it out, but she lifted her chin and said, 'If you're not interested—'

His hand tightened on hers. 'Oh, I'm interested. I just want to make sure you're not going to regret this in the morning and blame it on too much wine.'

Leila stared back, suppressing an urge to say *I'm blaming it on much more than that.* He wouldn't understand. 'I want this—even if it's just one night.'

Alix interlaced his fingers with hers. It felt like a shockingly intimate caress.

'It won't be one night, Leila, I can guarantee that.'

She shivered lightly. The way he said that sounded like a vow. Or a promise.

'Signor Alix...?'

He didn't even look at his friend. He just said, 'We're finished, Giorgio, thank you.'

But it was a long moment before Alix broke his gaze from hers and let go of her hand to stand up.

Leila couldn't remember much of leaving the restaurant, or of the boat ride along the magical Grand Canal at night. She was only aware of Alix's strong thighs beside hers on the seat, his arm tight around her shoulders, his hand resting disturbingly close to the curve of her breast.

She was only aware that she was finally leaving a part of her life behind and stepping into the unknown.

She couldn't believe she'd been so forward, and yet she knew that even if given a choice she wouldn't turn back now. This man had unlocked some deep secret part of her and she wanted to explore it. She didn't care about the fact that Alix Saint Croix was famous or rich or royalty. She was interested in the man. He called to her on a very basic level that no one had ever touched before.

And as the boat scythed through the choppy waters she reassured herself that she was going into this with eyes wide open. No romantic illusions. She was *not* starry-eyed any more. Pierre had seen to that when she'd let him woo her. That had been just after the death of her mother, when she'd been at her most vulnerable. She wasn't vulnerable any more. And Leila had no intention of shutting herself away like a nun for the rest of her life.

They were approaching a building now—another grand *palazzo*. A man stood on the small landing dock and threw a rope to the driver. They came alongside the wooden jetty and Alix jumped nimbly out of the boat before turning back to lift Leila out as easily as if she weighed nothing.

As he let her down on the jetty he kept her close to his body, and her eyes widened when she felt her belly brush against a very hard part of him. Her pulse quickened and between her legs she felt damp.

Then he turned, and held her hand as he strode through the open doors. Leila had to almost run to keep up and she tugged at his hand. He looked back, something stark etched onto his face. She refused to let it intimidate her.

'What is this place?'

'It belongs to a friend—he's away.'

'Oh...'

A petite older woman dressed in black approached

them and Alix exchanged some words with her in fluent Italian. It was only then that Leila looked around and took in the grandeur of the reception hall. The floor was marble, and there were massive stone columns stretching all the way up to a ceiling that was covered in very old-looking frescoes.

Then Alix was tugging her hand again and they were following the woman up the main staircase. The eyes from numerous huge stern portraits followed their progress and Leila superstitiously avoided looking at them, sensing a judgment she wasn't really blasé enough to ignore in spite of her bravado.

The corridor they walked into had thick carpet, muffling their footsteps. Massive ornate wooden doors were closed on each side. At the end of the corridor the woman came to some double doors and opened them wide, standing aside so they could go in.

Leila's breath stopped. It was the most stunningly sumptuous suite of rooms she'd ever seen. She let go of Alix's hand and walked over to where the glass French doors were open, leading out to a stone balcony overlooking a smaller canal.

She heard the door close softly and looked behind her to see Alix standing in the centre of the room, hands in his pockets, legs wide. Chest broad.

He took a hand out of his pocket and held it out. Silently Leila went to him, kicking off her sandals as she did so.

When she got to Alix, he drew her chiffon wrap off her shoulders and it drifted to the floor beside them. Then he reached around to the back of her head and removed the pin holding her hair up. It fell around her shoulders in a heavy silken curtain and he ran his hand through the strands.

'I wanted to do this the moment I saw you,' he said.

Feeling suddenly vulnerable, she blurted out, 'Did you

really not sleep with that woman after you pulled the curtains that night?'

His grey gaze bored into hers. 'No, I did not sleep with Carmen that night. I wouldn't lie to you about that, Leila.'

She found that she believed him, but she still had to battle the insidious suspicion that he would say whatever he wanted to get her into bed. Not that he'd had to say much—she'd all but begged him!

Furiously she blocked out the raising clamour of voices and reached up, touching her mouth to his. 'Take me to bed, Alix,' she whispered.

CHAPTER FIVE

AGAINST THE MUTED lighting of the opulent suite Alix looked every inch the powerful man he was. He took up so much space, and a sudden flutter of fear clutched at Leila's belly. Could she really handle a man like this?

But then he took her hand and led her into another room. The bedroom.

Its furnishings were ridiculously, gloriously lush. A four-poster, canopied bed stood in the centre of the room, surrounded by thick velvet drapes held back by decorative rings. Through the windows Leila could see the Grand Canal, and boats moving up and down. The curtains fluttered in the breeze and yet she was hot. Burning up.

Alix came and stood in front of her. Leila was at eye level with the middle of his chest. Never more than now had she been so aware of his sheer masculinity and strength. She wished she had the nerve to reach out and touch him, but she didn't. The boldness that had led her here seemed to be fleeing in the face of the stark reality facing her.

Alix tipped up her chin with a curled forefinger and Leila couldn't escape his gaze.

'We'll take this slow.'

Leila swallowed. So much for trying to repel him with her inexperience. His eyes burned. And something melted inside her at his consideration. He pulled her forward then, until her breasts were touching his body, her nipples tightening in reaction. Both his hands went to her jaw, caressing the delicate bone structure before tilting her face upwards. And then his head dipped and his mouth was over hers.

Leila made a soft sound in the back of her throat. His tongue explored along the seam of her mouth until she opened up to him, and then he was stroking her tongue intimately, teeth nipping at her full lower lip. Her hands curled into his shirt, clutching. He was all hard muscle and heat and he tasted of wine.

When Alix drew back after long, drugging moments, Leila followed him, opening her eyes slowly, all her senses colliding and melting into one throbbing beat of desire. She'd never imagined it could be like this. After just a kiss.

Alix brought his hands to the small buttons running down the front of her tunic. His skin was dark against the silk and Leila watched as slowly the front of her tunic fell open to reveal her lacy bra underneath.

'So beautiful…' breathed Alix as he saw her breasts revealed, more voluptuous than Leila had ever been comfortable with.

He slid a hand inside her tunic and cupped one, testing its shape, its firm weight. The effect on her body was so intensely pleasurable that Leila was too embarrassed to look at Alix. She ducked her head forward and her hair slipped over her shoulders, the ends touching his hand.

She gave a little gasp when Alix's other hand caught her hair at the back of her head and tugged gently. His fingers were squeezing her breast now, and her nipple was pinched tight with need. Leila wanted something but she wasn't sure what. *More.*

When he bent to take her mouth again she whimpered. And then his hand was pulling down the silk cup of her bra and he was palming her naked breast, fingers trapping her nipple, squeezing gently.

Alix's kiss was rougher than before, but Leila met it full-on, already feeling more confident, sucking his tongue deep, nipping his mouth. He was pushing her bra up now, over her breasts, freeing them. Pulling the top part of her tunic wide open.

When he eventually broke the kiss he was breathing harshly, eyes glittering like molten mercury.

There was something raw in his expression that made excitement mixed with sheer terror spike inside Leila. Alix moved back, tugging her with him, until he sat down on the edge of the massive bed.

Leila's breasts were exposed—framed by her pushed-up bra and the tunic. She should have felt self-conscious, but she didn't. Alix's gaze rested there and then he cupped one breast and brought his mouth to it, teasing the hard tip with his tongue before pulling it into his mouth and suckling.

Leila thought she might die. Right there and then. She'd never experienced anything so decadent, so delicious, as this hot, sucking heat. When he administered the same attention to her other breast her legs buckled and she landed on Alix's lap, his mouth and tongue lapping at her engorged flesh, making her squirm and writhe as a coil of tension wound higher and higher between her legs.

He broke away suddenly, his voice gruff. 'I need to see you.'

He carefully stood Leila up again and she felt momentarily dizzy, holding on to his arm to steady herself. He stood in front of her and slowly started to peel her tunic up and over her head. After a moment's hesitation Leila lifted her arms and it came all the way off, landing on the floor at their feet.

Then Alix deftly removed her twisted bra, and that disappeared too. Now she was naked apart from her trousers and underwear.

He was looking at her, eyes dark and unreadable. His hands were tracing her contours as reverently as if she was a piece of sculpted marble.

'I want to see you too.' Leila heard the words coming from her mouth and wasn't even aware of thinking them. *Dangerous.*

He dropped his hands and stood before her, silently inviting her to undress him. Leila lifted her hands to his shirt and slowly undid his buttons, his shirt falling open as she moved down his massive chest.

When she got to where his shirt was tucked into his trousers she hesitated for a moment, before pulling it free and undoing the last buttons. Soon it was open completely, and she pushed it wide open and off his shoulders. Alix opened his cufflinks, and then the shirt slid off completely.

Leila was in awe. The sleek strength of his muscles under the dark olive skin was fascinating to her. There was a little hair around his pectorals and a dark line down through his muscle-packed abdomen, disappearing enticingly into his trousers.

She reached out and put her hands on him, spread her fingers wide. His scent was hypnotising her…earthy and musky and *male*. The scent she'd made for him mixed with his own unique essence. She bent forward to press her lips against his hot skin, her mouth exploring and finding the small hard point of his nipple. She licked it experimentally and Alix jerked.

She pulled back, looked up. 'Did I hurt you?'

He shook his head and smiled. 'No, you didn't hurt me...*sorcière*. Lie down on the bed,' he instructed.

Leila was only too happy to comply. She felt shaky. The taste of his skin was addictive. She collapsed onto the bed and Alix moved over her before pressing a kiss to her mouth and moving down, trailing his lips over her jaw and neck, down to her breasts, anointing one and then the other.

He pulled back slightly and looked at her before saying, 'I'm going to take your trousers off...'

Leila bit her lip and then nodded. Her belly contracted when Alix's fingers came to her button and zip, undoing them both, and then he put his hands to the sides of her silk trousers to slide them down.

She lifted her hips to help. When they were off Alix's hands went to his own trousers, and with a swift economy of movement they were off too. Along with his underwear. He was now gloriously and unashamedly naked. Leila came up on her elbows, her eyes going wide at the sight of him.

His body was a honed mass of hard muscles and masculine contours. She'd never seen anything like it. All the way from his shoulders and chest, down to slim hips and strong muscled thighs. Between his thighs and lower belly was a thicket of dark hair, out of which rose the very core of his virility. Long and thick and hard. Proud.

As Leila watched he brought a hand to himself, stroking gently. It was so unbelievably sensual that her mouth dried even as other parts of her felt as if they were gushing with wet heat.

When he took his hand from himself Leila fell back against the soft covers of the bed. Alix reached forward and gently pulled her panties free of her hips and legs. Dropping them to the floor.

Now they were both naked, and Alix came alongside

her on the bed. She could feel his bold erection against her thigh. A potent invitation. But she was too shy to explore him there.

Instead, he kissed her—long, drugging kisses that sent her out of her mind completely as his hands explored her body, squeezing her buttocks, her breasts, following the contours of her waist and hips. And then he was pushing her legs apart and long fingers were exploring her *there*, where no one had ever touched her. Not even herself.

In a moment of panic at this intimate exploration she reached down and put a hand on his, stopping him. She looked at him, breath laboured, feeling hot.

One of Alix's thighs was between her legs and she could feel the heat of him there, very close to the apex of her legs, where his hand was. And as suddenly as she'd felt panic she felt an urgency she couldn't understand. She took her hand away again.

'I won't hurt you, Leila.' Alix promised. 'Any moment you want to stop, just say and I will.'

She nodded her head. 'Thank you...'

His hand started moving again, and when she felt him push one finger and then two inside her she let out a gasp, her head going back, eyes shut tight, as if that could control the almost violent reactions happening in her body.

He was moving his fingers in and out and she could feel how wet she was. His movements got faster and the heel of his hand pressed against a part of her that needed more friction. Without even realising she was doing it Leila lifted her hips, pushing into him, seeking more.

She was unaware of the smile of pure masculine satisfaction on Alix's face as he watched her.

There was something coiling so tight and deep within her that Leila begged incoherently for it to stop, or break, or do *something*. It was painful, but it was also the most exquisitely pleasurable thing she'd ever felt. And then suddenly her whole body was caught in the grip of a storm and she broke into a million pieces. She felt like the sun, the moon, stardust, pleasure and pain. All at once.

When her body was as lax as if someone had drained every bone out of it, she opened her eyes and blinked.

Alix looked vaguely incredulous. 'That was your first orgasm?'

Leila nodded faintly. She guessed it was. Living in such a small space with her mother hadn't exactly been conducive to normal female exploration. And then she'd been so grief-stricken and busy...

The expression on Alix's face changed from incredulous to intent. He moved so that his body lay between her legs, forcing them apart. Leila still felt sensitive down there, but as Alix moved against her subtly she found that excitement was growing again—a need for more even though *more* surely couldn't be possible...

Alix kissed her, surrounding her in his heat and strength. Leila moved her hands all over him—down his torso to his hips, his muscular buttocks. And all the while he was rocking against her gently, and that urgency was building in her again...for something...for *him*.

He pulled his mouth away from her breast and she could feel the tip of his erection nudging against her opening, sliding in tantalisingly.

'Are you okay?'

She nodded. She wasn't on earth any more. She was on some new and exotic planet where time and space had become immaterial. There was no real world any more.

'Yes,' she said out loud, so that there was no ambiguity.

Alix's jaw tightened. 'This might hurt at first... Stay with me—it'll get better, I promise.'

And with that he thrust in, deep into Leila's untried

flesh, stretching her wide. She gasped and arched against him, part in rejection of his invasion and part in awe at how right it felt in spite of the pain—which was blinding and red-hot. But she took a breath and looked into Alix's eyes, trusting him.

He was so big and heavy inside her. And then he moved—slowly, deeper. Pushing against her resistance. And then he pulled out again. Leila could feel sweat break out on her brow, between her breasts. She'd never thought sex would be so gritty, *base*.

Alix was relentless, moving in a little deeper each time, and as Leila's flesh got used to him, accommodated him better, the awful sting of pain faded, becoming something else. Something much more pleasurable. Even more pleasurable than before.

Something about Alix's urgency was transmitted to her and Leila instinctively wrapped her legs around him. She felt inordinately tender in that moment, cradling this huge man between her legs, feeling the force of him inside her body.

His movements got stronger, more powerful. And Leila's hips were moving, circling. He reached down between them and touched her *there*, close to where he was thrusting. Circling his thumb, making stars explode behind her eyes, making her body tight with need again.

She was gasping, her body arching against him, buttocks tightening as he pushed her to the very limit of her endurance and she fell again, down and down, from an even higher height than the first time.

She was coasting on such a wave of bliss that she was barely aware of Alix's own body, pumping hard into hers, before he too went taut and with a guttural groan exploded in a rush of heat inside her.

* * *

Leila came to when she felt herself being lifted out of the bed, pliant and weak. She managed to raise her head and open her eyes to see he was walking them into a dimly lit bathroom…acres of marble and golden fixtures.

Steam was rising from a sunken bath that looked big enough to swim in, and Alix knelt and gently deposited Leila into the pleasantly hot water.

She looked at him, properly awake now. 'What are you doing?'

He grimaced. 'You'll be sore…and you bled a little.'

Leila thought of the bed and the sumptuous sheets. Mortified, she said, 'Oh, no!'

Alix looked stern. 'It was my fault. I should have known to prepare…'

Another expression crossed his face then, something like dawning horror, but it was hard to see in the shadows of the room, and then it was gone, replaced by something indecipherable.

He stood up and Leila saw that he'd wrapped a towel around his waist. It still didn't disguise the healthy bulge underneath, though, and her face flamed as she sank down into the bubbles.

'I'll be back in a minute.'

Alix left the bathroom and Leila moved experimentally, wincing when she felt the sting of something between pleasure and pain between her legs. She ached too—all over. But pleasurably.

Letting her head fall back, she allowed the water to soothe her body. Her brain was foggy but one thing was crystal clear: she was no longer a virgin. She'd allowed Alix Saint Croix to be more intimate with her than anyone else. And it had felt…*amazing*. Stupendous. Transformative.

It was as if this body she'd had all her life was suddenly a new thing. Her hand moved of its own volition up over the flat plane of her belly and cupped her breast. Her nipple was roused to a hard peak under her hand, still slightly sensitive. When Leila brushed it a zing of pleasure went to her groin.

She felt emboldened—empowered. Like a woman for the first time in her life. That perfume she'd chosen earlier… she got it now. She could own a scent like that and wear it with sensual pride. Dreamily, she smiled, her hand over her breast, fingers trapping her nipple, squeezing gently as Alix had done…

Alix felt marginally more under control dressed in his trousers. Up until a couple of minutes ago he had felt as if someone had drugged him and he'd lost any sense of rationale or control. And he *had*. And about something so fundamentally important to him that he was still reeling.

But he was already becoming distracted again, losing focus. He stood in the doorway of the bathroom, watching Leila cup her breast in her hand, a small smile playing around her mouth, and just like that Alix was hard again, ready for her.

That first initial thrust into her body… It had been heaven and hell—because he'd known that while he was experiencing possibly the most exquisitely sensual moment of his life she'd been in pain. Even though he'd been as gentle as he could… And then, when that pain had faded from her eyes and her body had begun to move under his, Alix hadn't had a hope of retaining any sense at all. He'd become a slave to the dictates of his body and hers.

He'd had to push her over the edge—touching her intimately, taking advantage of her inexperience—because he'd known he couldn't wait for her completion.

And then he'd exploded. Inside her. Without any barrier of protection.

Alix curbed the panic. Stepped into the bathroom. 'How are you feeling now?'

Leila immediately dropped her hand from her breast and tensed, opening her eyes, her smile fading. But then it came back...shyly.

'I'm okay. I think.'

Alix reached for a towel and held it out. Leila stood up and Alix couldn't help watching as the water sluiced down her perfect body. Her skin was like silk. She was exquisite. Slim and yet all woman, with full hips and breasts. Alix gritted his jaw to stop thinking about how it had felt to be cradled by her hips and thighs. How right it had felt. Right enough to send him mad—to make him forget important things. Like protection.

Leila rubbed herself dry with the towel, avoiding his eye now, and then Alix offered her a robe. She turned her back to him to put her arms into it and when she turned around again, belting it, she looked worried.

'Is something wrong?'

Alix felt a weight on his chest. Her eyes were so huge, so green. So innocent.

'Come into the bedroom. I asked the housekeeper to send some food and drinks up.'

He took her hand and led her out. A table was set up near the window. A candle flickered in the dim light. The sounds of the canal lapping against the building came faintly from outside.

They sat down and Leila looked even more worried. 'What is it, Alix? You're scaring me... '

'We didn't use protection.' He grimaced. 'That is, *I* didn't think of it. I presume you're not on any form of contraception?'

Leila shook her head, damp tendrils of dark hair slipping over her shoulders. Her cheeks coloured. 'No...I didn't think of it either.'

Alix's voice was harsh. 'It was my responsibility.'

She avoided his eyes for a long moment, and then she looked back at him. 'I think I'm okay, though. It's not a fertile time in my cycle. I've just finished a period.'

Something eased in his chest even as something else pierced him. A sense of loss. *Strange.*

He took her hand. 'I wasn't thinking. Ordinarily I never forget. And I can't *afford* to forget...'

He saw when comprehension dawned in those huge eyes.

Leila pulled her hand back. Her voice was stilted. 'Of course. A man like you has to be more careful than most. I understand.'

Alix felt a bizarre urge to say something to reassure her, to tell her that it was nothing personal. But he couldn't. Because it was true. He would have to father an heir with his Queen and no one else. His own father had created a storm of controversy by bedding numerous mistresses, who had all come forward at one time or another claiming to have had children by him.

It had been one of the many reasons the people of Isle Saint Croix had become so disillusioned with their King and overthrown him.

'It won't happen again, Leila. I'm sorry.'

Her eyes snapped back to his and Alix quirked a smile. 'I don't mean *that.* We *will* be doing that again, I just won't forget about protection again.'

Food lay on the table between them, unnoticed, and Alix forced himself to try and retain a modicum of civility. He held up a piece of cheese. 'Are you hungry?'

Leila shook her head and then looked away, embarrassed.

Alix reached across and took her chin, tipping it up. He smiled. 'But you *are* hungry for something…?'

It entranced Alix that she seemed to have no sense of guile, or of playing the coquette. And why would she? She'd been a virgin. Her gaze dropped to his mouth and he saw the same insatiable appetite that had been awoken inside himself. His body hummed and soared with it.

She nodded, telling him silently what she was hungry for. Alix wanted to groan. 'But you're going to be too sore…'

Leila shook her head, her eyes on his now. Feminine and full of that innate knowledge that a man couldn't possibly ever fathom. Amazing that she already had it. Alix had never really noticed it before now, because he'd never seen it as a spontaneous thing. The women he was usually with were all too cynical even to attempt it.

'I'm okay. Really.'

Her husky words took him out of his reverie. He needed no further encouragement, so he dropped the food, stood up and led Leila back over to the bed.

When Leila woke up again it was morning. She opened her eyes and saw that the room was bathed in sunlight. She was on her own. But just as she thought that, Alix strolled out of the bathroom, straightening his tie. He was impeccably dressed. Shaved. Cleaned up. When Leila felt utterly wanton.

She sat up and clutched the sheet to her body, thoroughly disorientated. Alix leaned against one of the four posters of the bed and crossed his arms. A sexy smile played around his mouth. 'You look adorable… all mussed up.'

Leila scowled, and then grew hot when she thought of how *mussed up* she'd become when Alix had taken her to bed for the second time. Somehow in the dimly lit bathroom and bedroom last night it had been easier to face this man. Now it was daylight, and a return to reality and sanity was here. And it was not welcome.

Twinges and aches made her wince as she leant out to the side of the bed to look for some clothes.

Alix was there in seconds. 'Are you okay?'

Leila looked at him and couldn't breathe. 'I'm fine... What time is it?'

She had no clue what the etiquette of this kind of morning-after scenario was. A morning-after in *Venice,* after a night of more debauchery than she'd ever known she was capable of. Mortification washed through her in a wave.

Alix glanced at his watch, oblivious to her inner turmoil. 'It's after ten. I'm sorry about this, but I do need to get back to Paris for a lunchtime meeting.'

Leila forced herself to meet his eyes, even though she wanted to slither down under the covers and all the way to Middle Earth. 'Of course. I need to get back too.'

Alix put his hands either side of her hips, effectively trapping her. 'You're not regretting anything, are you?'

His face was so close she could see the lighter flecks of grey in his eyes. And she knew that no matter how embarrassed she was right now, how gauche she felt, she really didn't regret a thing.

She shook her head and he pressed a firm kiss to her mouth before pulling back.

'Good. The housekeeper has sent up some breakfast, and I had some clothes sent over for both of us.'

'You did?' Leila boggled.

Alix shrugged and stood up. 'Sure—I called my assistant in Paris and she got them sent from a boutique here in Venice.'

Of course, Leila thought wryly to herself. She'd almost forgotten for a moment who Alix was. The power he wielded. The ease with which he clicked his fingers and had his orders obeyed. The ease with which she'd fallen into bed with him...

She had to stop thinking about that.

Galvanising herself, Leila got out of bed and pulled the sheet off the bed, tucking it around her body, all the while acutely aware of Alix's amused gaze.

'I'll have a quick shower,' she said, and walked to the bathroom with as much dignity as she could while trailing a long length of undoubtedly expensive Egyptian cotton behind her.

Once in the bathroom, Leila could hear Alix's phone ring and his deep tones as he answered. It was a welcome reminder that he was itching to move on, to get back to Paris and his life. And she needed to get on too.

As she stepped under the hot spray of the shower she told herself that if all she had was this night in Venice with a beautiful exiled king then she would be happy with that.

She valiantly ignored the physical pang in the region of her chest that told her otherwise. She was *not* her mother, and she was *not* going to fall for the first man she'd slept with.

An hour later they were back on Alix's private jet, taking off from Venice. Alix was talking in low tones in another guttural language on his phone. She guessed it must be a form of Spanish. It was a relief not to have his attention on her for a moment.

Leila looked out of the window and took a shaky

breath. Hard to believe her world had changed so irrevocably within less than twenty-four hours.

She wore the new clothes Alix's staff had sent over. Beautifully cut slim-fitting trousers and a loose long-sleeved silk top, with a wrap-around cashmere cardigan in the most divine sapphire-blue colour.

They'd even sent over fresh underwear and flat shoes. She felt cossetted and looked after. *Dangerous*. Because he did this sort of thing with women all the time.

When they'd been eating breakfast, just a short while before, she'd caught him looking at her intently. 'What?' Leila had asked. 'Have I got something on my face?'

Without make-up she'd felt bare. Exposed.

Alix had shaken his head. 'No. You're beautiful.'

And then he'd reached for her hand and she hadn't been able to look away from him.

'I want to see you again. Today...tonight. Tomorrow.'

Her heart had stopped, and then started again at twice the pace. 'But this was just one night...'

Wasn't it?

That was how she'd justified her outrageous behaviour. It had been a moment out of time.

Alix had looked a little fierce. 'Is one night enough for you?'

Trapped in his steely gaze, she'd asked herself if she could do this. Agree to an affair with this man? Have more of him? *Yes*, a pleading voice had answered.

Would he even let her go after she'd acquiesced so spectacularly? She knew the answer. Slowly she'd shaken her head. It wasn't enough for her either. She wanted more—shamelessly.

Alix's fingers had tightened around hers. 'Well, then...'

And now here she was, hurtling back towards the real world and a liaison she wasn't sure she knew how to navigate. She heard Alix terminate his call and thought of the dress he'd bought for her to go to the opera, and these new clothes.

She turned away from the view and found him looking at her. Before she could lose her nerve she said quickly, 'I don't want to be your mistress. I appreciate the clothes this morning, but I don't want you to buy me anything else.'

He looked at her for a moment, as if he truly couldn't understand what she was saying, and then he shrugged nonchalantly. 'Fine.'

Leila thought of something else and felt the cold hand of panic clutch at her gut. The prospect of press intrusion. Being photographed with Alix. It would inevitably bring scrutiny, and she did not want that under any circumstances.

She said, 'We can't go out in public. I don't want to end up in the papers. I'm not prepared for that kind of intrusion.'

Alix straightened, and something flashed across his face—surprise?—before it was masked and Leila thought she might have imagined it.

'I have an entire team at my disposal. I will make sure you're protected.'

Leila looked at him. She thought of Ricardo…and of the fact that Alix had been in and out of her shop a few times now and no one seemed to have picked up on it. Maybe it would be okay. Maybe the skeletons in her closet wouldn't jump out to bite her.

She forced a smile. 'Okay.'

CHAPTER SIX

'EARTH TO ALIX...HELLO? Anyone home?'

Alix blinked and looked at his friend and chief advisor, Andres, who had flown in from Isle Saint Croix to meet him. Andres was Alix's secret weapon. Devoutly loyal to getting Alix back on the throne, he was also working as a spy, of sorts, in the current regime in Isle Saint Croix. He was the reason Alix was going to get reinstated as King.

'Have you heard a word I've said?'

Alix knew he hadn't. His head had been consumed with soft silky skin. Long dark hair. Huge green eyes like jewels. Soft gasps and moans. The heady rush of pleasure when he— *Damn*. He jerked up out of his chair. This was ridiculous.

Leila was like a fever in his blood. He couldn't concentrate.

He went and stood at the window, and then after a few seconds turned back to his friend and said, 'I've met someone new.'

Andres made a small whistling sound, his boyishly handsome face cracking into a wry grin. 'I know you move fast, Alix, but this is your fastest ever. Usually you leave at least a week between switching partners. This is good, though—when will we see pictures hit the press?'

Alix folded his arms and scowled at his friend's exaggeration. And then he thought of what Leila had said about wanting to avoid press intrusion. And, as much as he needed it right now, suddenly the thought of paparazzi hounding her was very unpalatable. It made him feel almost...*protective*.

There had to be a solution. His brain seized on an idea and it took root. And the more it did so, the more seductive it became.

'Our supporters on the ground are aware that we are conducting a campaign of misdirection, aren't they?'

Andres nodded. 'Absolutely. They know that you're primed and ready to return, no matter what the press says.'

'Then if I was to leave and go to my island in the Caribbean for ten days it could only work in our favour?'

Andres huffed out a breath. 'Well, sure... I mean, you're just as contactable there as here... And if there are photos emerging of you frolicking in the sun with some leggy beauty the opposition will be taken completely by surprise when we pull the rug right out from underneath them.'

Alix smiled, sweet anticipation flooding his blood. 'My thoughts exactly.'

Andres frowned. 'But, Alix, you do know that your island is totally impenetrable by the outside world? No paparazzi have ever caught you there. It's too far—too remote.'

Alix's smile faded as he got serious. 'Which is why you're going to arrange for one of my most trustworthy staff on the island to take long-range grainy photos—I'll let you know when is a good time. Enough to identify me, but not Leila. He can email them to you, and you can send them out to whoever you think should get them for maximum beneficial exposure. I want this controlled.'

Alix felt only the smallest pang of his conscience and told himself he'd still be protecting her identity.

Andres's eyes gleamed with unmistakable interest at the lengths his friend was willing to go to for a woman, but Alix cut him off before he could say anything.

'I don't want to discuss her, Andres, just set it up. We'll fly out tomorrow.'

'You want to take me *where*?'

The blinds were down in Leila's shop and she'd just closed up for the evening when Alix had appeared, causing a seismic physical response. She hadn't heard from him since that morning, when they'd arrived back from Venice, and she didn't like to admit the way her nerves had stretched tighter and tighter over the day, as she'd wondered if she'd hear from him again. In spite of what he'd said.

And now he was here, and he'd just said—

'I have an island in the Caribbean. It's private... secluded. I've cleared my schedule for the next ten days— I need to take a break. I want you to come with me, Leila. I want to explore this with you...what's going on between us.'

Leila felt sideswiped, bewildered, along with an illicit flutter of excitement. 'But...I can't just *leave*! Who'll look after my shop and business? The last thing I can afford now is to close up.'

Smoothly Alix said, 'I can hire someone to manage the shop in your absence. They won't have your knowledge, obviously, but they'll be able to cover basic sales till you get back.'

Leila opened her mouth to protest, but the truth was she wasn't really in a position to take orders for new perfumes until she found some factory space, so all she was doing in essence was selling what they had. She could mix perfumes on a very small scale, which was what she'd done for Alix. So she was dispensable.

Weakly, she protested. 'But we've only spent one night together. I can't just take off like this.'

Alix raised a brow. 'Can't you? What's stopping you?'

Leila felt irritation rise. 'Not everyone lives in a world where you can just take off to the other side of the earth on a whim. Some of us have to think of the consequences.' But right then Leila knew she wasn't thinking of financial or economic consequences—she was thinking of more emotional ones. Already.

Then Alix did the one thing guaranteed to scramble her brain completely. He came close and slid his hand around the back of her neck, under her hair, and tugged her towards him.

He said softly, 'I'll show you the consequences.'

His scent reached her brain before she even registered the effect it was having on her. Her blood started fizzing, and between her legs she was still tender but she could feel herself growing damp.

An acute physical reaction to desire. To this man.

Hunger, ravenous and scary, whipped through her so fast she couldn't control it. And when Alix lowered his mouth to hers she was already lost. Already saying yes, throwing caution to the wind. Because the truth was that dealing with him in this environment was scarier—so maybe going to the other side of the world would keep them in fantasy land. And when it was over she'd come back to normality. Whatever normal was...

When the kiss ended they were both breathing heavily, and Leila was pressed between the counter and Alix's very hard body. They looked at each other.

Shakily, Leila said, 'This is just... It won't last.' She didn't even frame it as a question.

Something infinitely hard came into Alix's eyes and he shook his head. He almost looked sad for a moment. 'No, it never lasts.'

Leila drew in a slightly shaky breath. One more step over the line couldn't hurt, could it? She was doing this with her eyes wide open. No illusions. No falling in love. She was not her innocent, naive mother.

'Okay, I'll come with you.'

Alix just smiled.

'There it is—just down there.'

Leila looked, and couldn't quite believe her eyes. She'd never seen such vivid colours. Lush green and pale white sand, clear azure water. Palm trees. It was like the manifestation of a dream she wasn't even aware she'd had.

She couldn't actually speak. She was dumbfounded. This was the last in a series of flights that had taken them from Paris to Nassau and now in a smaller plane to Alix's private island, which was called Isle de la Paix—Island of Peace.

And it looked peaceful from up here. They were circling lower now, and Leila could see a beautiful colonial-style house, and manicured grounds leading down to a long sliver of beach where foamy waves lapped the pristine shore.

She was glad she'd agreed to come here—because she knew this experience would help her to keep Alix in some fantasy place once their affair was over.

They landed, bouncing gently over a strip cut into the grass in a large open, flat area. Leila could see a couple of staff waiting outside and an open-top Jeep.

When they left the plane the warmth hit Leila like a

hot oven opening in her face. It was humid—and delicious. She could already feel the effects sinking through her skin to her bones, making them more fluid, less tense.

The smiling staff greeted them with lilting voices and took their bags into a van. Alix led Leila over to the Jeep, taking her by the hand. When he'd buckled her in, and climbed in at the other side, he looked at her and grinned.

Leila grinned back, her heart light. He suddenly looked more carefree than she'd ever seen him, and she realised that he'd always looked slightly stern. Even when relaxed. But not here.

'Would you like a brief tour of the island, madam?'

'That would be lovely,' Leila responded with another grin.

They took off, and Alix drove them along dirt tracks through the lush forest that skirted along the most beautiful beaches she'd ever seen. The sun hit them and the Jeep with dappled rainbows of light, bathing them in warmth. Leila tipped her head back and closed her eyes, revelling in the sensation.

When the Jeep came to a stop she opened her eyes again and saw that they were on the edge of a small, perfect beach.

Leila leant forward. The smell of the sea was heady, along with the sharper tang of vegetation and dry earth. She itched to analyse the scents but the view competed. It was sensory overload. And the most perfectly hued clear seawater she'd ever seen lapped the shore just yards away.

Alix jumped out of the Jeep and came around, expertly unbuckling her belt and lifting her out before she could object, strong arms under her legs and back. He walked them down to the beach. It was late afternoon, and still hot, but the intense heat of the sun had diminished.

He put her down and looked at her, raising a brow. 'Have you ever skinny-dipped?'

Leila's mouth opened and she blustered, 'No, I certainly have *not*!' even as she felt a very illicit tingle of rebellion.

Alix was already pulling off his clothes. He'd changed on the plane before they'd got to Nassau, into a polo shirt and casual trousers. Leila gaped as his body was revealed, piece by mouthwatering piece.

She'd only seen him naked in the dimly lit confines of the Venetian *palazzo*, and now he stood before her, lit by the glorious sun against a paradise backdrop.

He was stunning. Not an ounce of fat. Hewn from rock. Pure olive-skinned muscular beauty. And one muscle in particular was twitching under her rapt gaze.

Leila's cheeks flamed and she dragged her gaze up. She sounded strangled. 'I can't—we can't! What if someone comes along?' She glanced behind her into the trees.

But then Alix was in front of her, his hand turning her chin back to him. She looked at him helplessly and he said, 'Listen. Just listen.'

Leila did—and heard nothing. Not one sound that didn't come directly from the island itself. No sirens or traffic or voices. Just the breeze and the trees and birds, and the water lapping near their feet.

'It's just us, Leila. Apart from a handful of staff at the house, we're completely alone.'

A sense of freedom such as she'd never felt before made her chest swell and lightness pervade her body. She felt young and carefree. It was heady.

'Now, are you coming into the water willingly? Or do I have to throw you in fully clothed?'

Leila started to shrug off her jacket, and said, mock petulantly, 'Fine, Your Majesty.'

Alix watched her, stark naked and completely blasé. 'That's more like it.'

His eyes got darker as Leila self-consciously took off her shirt and trousers, very aware of their chain-store dullness.

When she was in her bra and pants she hesitated, and Alix growled softly, 'Keep going.'

Leila fought back the memory of that other woman and reached behind her to undo her bra, letting it fall forward and off. The bare skin of her breasts prickled and her nipples tightened. Avoiding Alix's gaze now, she pulled down her pants with an economic movement, stepping out of them and laying them neatly on her pile of clothes.

She was naked on a beach, in a tropical paradise with an equally naked man. The reality was too much to take in, so with a whoop of disbelief and sheer joy Leila ran for the sea, feeling the warm, salty water embrace her. And then she dived deep under an oncoming wave before she exploded into pieces completely.

Leila wandered through Alix's house dressed in nothing but one of his oversized T-shirts, her hair in a tangled knot on top of her head. She'd never been so consistently un-dressed in her life, and after her initial self-consciousness she'd realised to her shock that she was something of a sensualist, relishing the freedom. Much as she'd exulted in the feel of her naked body in the sea on that first day.

Since they'd arrived at his house after skinny-dipping three days before, damp and salty from the sea, they'd barely left his bedroom. He'd retrieved food from the kitchen at intermittent intervals, and they'd gorged on each other in a feast of the senses. Leila's inexperience was fast becoming a thing of the past under Alix's ex-pert tutelage.

When Leila had woken a short time before it had been the first time Alix hadn't been in bed beside her, or in the shower, or bringing food back to the bedroom. So she'd come to find him.

And now she was taking in the splendour of his house properly for the first time. It was luxurious without being ostentatious. Mostly in tones of soothing off-white and grey. Muslin drapes billowed in the soft island breeze through open windows. It truly was paradise, and Leila felt a pang that her mother was gone and couldn't experience this.

Little *objets d'art* were dotted here and there—tastefully. Leila stopped before a small portrait that hung in the main foyer area and her jaw dropped when she realised she must be looking at an original Picasso.

A soft sound from nearby made Leila whirl around, and her face flamed when she saw an attractive middle-aged, casually dressed woman looking at her with a warm smile on her face.

The woman put out a hand. 'Sorry to startle you, Miss Verughese. I was wondering if you'd like some lunch? I'm Matilde—Alix's roving housekeeper.'

She had an American accent. Leila forced an embarrassed smile. She hadn't seen any staff yet. She gestured to her clothes—or lack of them. 'Sorry, I was just looking for Mr Saint—that is… Alix.'

Matilde smiled wider. 'Don't worry, honey, that's what this island is all about—relaxation. You'll find Alix in his study, just down the hall. Why don't I prepare a nice lunch for you both on the terrace? It'll be ready in about half an hour.'

Leila smiled back at the woman, who was clearly friendly enough with Alix to be on first-name terms. 'Please call me Leila—and that sounds lovely.'

The woman was turning away, and then she turned back suddenly and said, *sotto voce* to Leila, 'You know, he's never brought a woman here before.'

And then, with a wink, she was disappearing down the corridor, leaving Leila with a belly full of butterflies. She hated it that it made her so happy to know this wasn't routine for him.

Leila wandered down the hall, with its gleaming polished wooden floors. She heard a low, deep voice and followed it into a room to see Alix, bare-chested, sitting at a desk with a laptop open before him. He was on the phone. And he was frowning.

The room was as beautiful as the rest of the house, with floor-to-ceiling shelves filled with books. Books that looked well used.

He looked up and saw her, and some indecipherable expression crossed his face before he said something Leila couldn't hear and put down the phone. He closed his laptop.

Leila felt as if she'd intruded on something and put out a hand. 'Sorry. I didn't mean to disturb you.'

Alix stood up and Leila saw that he was wearing only low-slung, faded jeans. Her insides sizzled. He looked amazing in a suit and tuxedo, but like this…he was edible.

'You're not disturbing me. Sorry for leaving you…'

He came and stood before her and Leila imagined she could feel the electricity crackle between them.

'I bumped into Matilde,' she babbled. 'She seems lovely. She's making us lunch and it'll be on the terrace in half an—'

Alix put a finger to Leila's mouth and quirked a sexy smile. 'Half an hour?'

Leila nodded.

Alix took his hand away and scooped Leila up into his

arms before she knew what was happening. He was soon climbing up the stairs and Leila hissed, 'She's making lunch, Alix. We can't just disappear—'

They were at the bedroom door by now, and the sight of the tumbled bed made Leila stop talking. Apparently they *could*.

When they finally did make it down to the terrace, much later that day, Matilde was totally discreet and delivered a feast of tapas-like food. Salads and pasta. American-style wings and ribs. Seafood—spicy fish and rice, crab claws with garlic sauce. Lobster. Chilled white wine.

Leila had wondered if they would even make a dent in the feast laid before them, but just when she was licking her fingers after eating spicy fish she caught Alix's amused gaze.

'What?'

He leant forward. 'You have some sauce on the corner of your lip.'

Leila darted out her tongue and encountered Alix's finger, because he'd reached out to scoop it up. Immediately a wanton carnality entered Leila's blood and she moved so that she could suck Alix's finger into her mouth, swirling her tongue around the tip, much as he'd shown her how to—

She let his finger go with an abrupt *pop*, aghast at how easily she was becoming a slave to this man and her desires.

She found herself blurting out the first thing that came into her head to try and diffuse the intensity. 'Is it true that you've never brought a woman here?' She immediately regretted her words. Damn her runaway mouth!

Hurriedly she said, 'It's okay. You don't have to answer that—it doesn't matter.'

Alix's voice was wry. 'I should have known Matilde couldn't resist. She's a romantic at heart after all—as I think are *you*, Leila.'

She looked at Alix, horror flooding her at the thought that he might think— She shook her head. She forced all the boneless, mushy feelings out of her body and head and said firmly, 'No, I'm not. I'm a realist, and I know what this is—a moment in time. And I'm fine with that—believe me.'

Alix looked at Leila in the flickering candlelight. The island was soft and fragrant around them. *Like her.* Apparently he didn't need to be worried that she'd got the wrong idea from Matilde, and he wasn't sure why that thought wasn't giving him more of a sense of comfort. What? Did he *want* her to be falling for him?

She had her profile towards him and he was stunned all over again at her very regal beauty. Totally unadorned and all the more astounding because of it. In the last couple of days her skin had lost its pale glow and become more rich. Her Indian heritage was obvious, giving her that air of exotic mystery. Her green eyes stood out even more.

He felt a pang of guilt when he recalled the conversation he'd had with Andres to set up the photo opportunity. It would be a far less intrusive photo than most of those he'd had taken with other women, so why did he feel so uncomfortable about it? And guilty…?

It didn't help to ease his conscience when Leila looked at him then and he couldn't read the expression on her face or in her eyes. It irritated him—as if she'd retreated behind a shield.

'Do you think you'll ever regain your throne in Isle Saint Croix?'

Alix blinked, jerked unceremoniously back to reality.

Immediately he was suspicious—but then he felt ridiculous. She wasn't some spy from Isle Saint Croix, sent to find out his movements.

Even so, Alix had kept his motivation secret for so long that he wasn't about to bare his soul to anyone—even her.

He shrugged nonchalantly. 'Perhaps some day. If the political situation improves enough for me to make a bid for the throne again... But there is a lot of anger still—at my father.'

Leila had turned more towards him now, and put her elbows on the table, resting her chin on one hand. The diaphanous robe she was wearing made it easy to see the outline of her perfect braless breasts and Alix was immediately distracted. He had to drag his mind out of a very carnal place.

'What was he like?'

The question was softly, innocently asked, and yet it aroused an immediate sense of rage in Alix. He felt restless, and got up to stand at the nearby railing that protected the terrace and looked down over the lawns below.

He heard Leila shift in her seat. 'I'm sorry. If you don't want to talk about it...'

But he found that he did. Here in one of the quietest corners of the earth. With her.

He didn't turn around. Tightly he said, 'My father was corrupt—pure and simple. He grew up privileged and never had to ask for anything. It ruined him. His own father was a good ruler, but weak. He let my father run amok. By the time my father married my mother—who was an Italian princess from an ancient Venetian family line—he was out of control. The country was falling apart, but he didn't notice the growing poverty or dissent. My mother didn't endear herself to the people either. She spent more time gadding around the world than on the island—in Paris, or London, or New York.'

Alix turned around and leant back against the railing. He looked down into his wine glass and swirled the liquid. When he looked at Leila again she was rapt, eyes huge. It made something in Alix's chest tight.

'My father took mistresses—local girls, famous beauties, it made no difference. He had them in the castle whether my mother was there or not. I think her attitude was that once she'd given him his heir and a spare she could do what she wanted.'

Leila said softly, 'You had a younger brother...?'

Alix nodded. 'Yes—Max.'

He went on.

'One day, both my parents were in residence—which was a rare enough occurrence. A young local girl was trying to see my father, holding a baby, crying. Her baby was ill and she needed help. She was claiming that it was his—which was quite probable. My father had his soldiers throw her and the baby out of the castle...'

Alix's mouth twisted.

'What he didn't realise was that a mob had gathered outside, and when they saw this they attacked. Our own soldiers were soon colluding with the crowd and they turned on my father and mother. They shot my parents and my brother, but I got away.'

Alix deliberately skated over the worst of it—made it sound less horrific than it had been.

He drank the rest of his wine in one gulp.

Leila's eyes shone with what looked suspiciously like tears. It had a profound effect on Alix.

'Your brother...were you close to him?'

He nodded. 'The closest. Everything I do now is to avenge his death and to make sure it's not in vain.'

He knew instantly that he'd said too much when Leila frowned slightly. Clearly she was wondering how his living the life of a louche royal playboy tallied with avenging his brother's untimely death.

She didn't know, of course, of the charitable foundations he headed that supported the families of people who'd lost relatives in traumatic circumstances. Or the amount of times he'd gone on peace and reconciliation missions all over the world, observing how it was done so he'd be qualified to apply it to his own country when he returned.

Leila looked at Alix, so tall and brooding in the moonlight. Her heart ached for him—for the young boy he'd been, helpless, watching his own parents destroy their legacy—and taking his younger brother with them.

She thought of how she'd lied about her father being dead and it made her feel dishonest now, after he'd told her what had happened to him.

'Alix,' she began, 'there's something I should—'

But he cut Leila off as he moved, coming over to the table. He put his glass down. His eyes were blazing and she could see they'd dropped to her breasts, unfettered beneath her thin gown. Instantly heat sizzled in her veins and she forgot what she'd wanted to say.

'I think we've talked enough for one evening. I want you, Leila.' And then, almost as an afterthought, he said, 'I need you.'

I need you. Those three words set Leila's blood alight. She sensed that he needed to lose himself after telling her what he had. So she stood up, allowing him to see all of her, thinly veiled. He might have said he needed her, but she knew that this was about *this*.

And as Alix led her inside and up to the bedroom she reassured herself once again that that was fine.

* * *

'Who would have thought you like to read American *noir* crime novels?' Leila's voice was teasing as she lay draped across Alix's chest on a large sun lounger in his garden.

He lowered his book and looked at her, arching a brow. 'And that *you* would like Matilde's collection of historical romance novels covered with half-naked Neanderthals and long, flowing blonde hair?'

Leila giggled and ducked her head, and then looked up again. 'It was my mother's fault. She devoured them and led me astray from a young age.'

'You must miss her.'

Leila unpeeled herself from Alix and sat up, pulling her knees to her chin and wrapping her arms around them. She looked out over the stunning view from their elevated height in the garden at the back of the house, where the pool was.

Quietly, Leila said, 'I miss her, of course. It was always just the two of us.'

Leila was afraid to look at Alix in case he saw the emotion she was feeling. A mix of grief and happiness. And gratitude to be in this place. To be with this man and yet to know not to expect more. Even if her heart *did* give a little lurch at that.

Alix came up on one elbow beside her, his long half-naked body stretched out in her peripheral vision like a mouthwatering temptation.

'The man you were with before—what did he do to you?'

Leila glanced at him. *Damn*. She'd forgotten that she'd mentioned Pierre, even in passing. She shrugged. 'He was a mistake. I was naive.'

'How?'

Leila bit her lip, and then said, 'It was just after my

mother died—I was vulnerable. He paid me attention. I believed him when he said he just wanted to get to know me, that he wouldn't push me. But one night he came up to my apartment and said he was tired of waiting for me to put out. He tried to force himself on me—'

Alix sprang upright in one fluid move and caught Leila's arm, turning her to face him. Anger was blazing from his eyes. 'Did he hurt you?'

Leila was shocked at this display of emotion. 'No. He… he tried to, but I had some mace. I threatened to use it on him. So he just insulted me and left.'

'*Dieu*…Leila…he could have—'

'I know,' Leila said sharply. 'But he didn't. Thank God. And I was proved a fool for believing that he—'

Alix's hand tightened on her arm. 'No, you weren't a fool. You just wanted reassurance and some attention.'

Words trembled on Leila's lips. Words about how much she'd wanted to believe that love and security did exist. *Could* exist. But she couldn't let them spill. Not here, with this man. He'd made no promises. He was offering her this slice of paradise—that was all and if she'd been foolish before she'd be triply so if she started dreaming about anything more with a man like Alix.

He urged her gently back down onto the lounger and pushed their books aside. Tugging her over his chest again, he cupped the back of her head, fingers threading through her hair. 'The man was an idiot, Leila.'

He brought her mouth down to meet his and they luxuriated in a long and explicit kiss. Leila felt emotional—as if Alix was silently communicating his gratitude to her for trusting enough in him to let him be the one to take her innocence.

The kiss got hotter, more desperate. Alix's free hand deftly untied the strings of her bikini and she felt the flimsy material being pulled from between their bodies. Then his hand was smoothing down her back, cupping her buttock and squeezing gently, and then more firmly, long fingers covering the whole cheek, exploring close to where the seam of her body was wet and hot.

Obeying the clamouring of her blood, Leila moved over Alix so that her legs straddled his hips, breasts pressed to his broad chest. With an expert economy of movement, barely breaking their connection, mouths and body, Alix managed to extricate himself from his shorts and disposed of Leila's bikini bottoms too. Now there were no barriers between them.

Leila had got so used to their privacy being respected that she felt completely uninhibited. Her legs were spread and she could feel him, hard and potent, at her buttocks. Alix moved so that his erection was between them, and Leila luxuriated in moving her body up and down, her juices anointing his shaft, making him groan…making them both want more.

Until she couldn't stand teasing him any more and rose up, biting her lip as Alix donned protection, and then letting her breath out in a long hiss as he joined their bodies and he was deep inside her. Nothing existed in the world except this moment. This exquisite climb to the top of ecstasy.

CHAPTER SEVEN

ALIX HAD HIS HANDS in his pockets and he was looking out over one of the back lawns to where Leila was deep in conversation with his head gardener. He smiled and realised that in spite of the fact that he was standing on the precipice of possibly the most tumultuous period of his life he'd never felt so calm…or content.

The last ten days had been unlike anything he'd ever experienced. He'd never spent so much time alone with a woman. Not even the woman he'd thought he'd lost his heart to all those years ago. That had been youthful lust mixed up with folly and arrogance and hurt pride.

Leila was easy to talk to. *Disturbingly* easy to talk to. He'd told her things that he'd never discussed with anyone else. Not even Andres.

And their chemistry was still white-hot. Alix frowned. He knew he had to let Leila go. Within days the news was going to break that Alix's people had voted for him to return to Isle Saint Croix. His life would not be his own any more. And he couldn't return to the island with a mistress. It would undo all his hard work. He had to return alone, and then find a wife.

He felt heavy inside, all of a sudden. And then Leila looked up and spotted him, a smile spreading across her face. She said something to the gardener and shook his hand. The old man looked comically delighted with himself and Alix shook his head. *The Leila effect.* Yesterday he'd found her in the kitchen, showing Matilde how to make a genuine hot Indian vegetarian curry.

She hurried towards him now with a box in her hand, dressed for travelling in slim-fitting trousers and a sleeveless cashmere top. He drank her in greedily…something elemental inside him growled hungrily. He wasn't ready to let her go—and yet how could he keep her?

'I'm sorry. I didn't mean to keep you waiting.'

Alix smiled even as an audacious idea occurred to him. 'You didn't. Was Lucas helpful?'

Leila smiled. 'Amazingly! He's even given me some flower cuttings to take home in special preservative bags. I've never smelled anything like them. If I can just distil their essences somehow—' She broke off, embarrassed. 'Sorry—we should get going, shouldn't we?'

Alix's chest felt tight. 'Yes, we should. The plane is waiting.'

'I'll just get my handbag.'

Leila moved to go inside, but then stopped beside Alix and looked up at him. Her voice was husky. 'Thank you… this has been truly magical.'

He reached out and cupped her jaw, running his thumb across the fullness of her lower lip. 'Yes, it has,' he agreed.

And right then he knew that he wasn't ready to let Leila go, and that whatever it took to keep that from happening, he would do it.

'Stay with me tonight?'

Leila looked at Alix across the back seat of his chauffeur-driven car. It was very late—after midnight—and the rain-wet streets of Paris were like an alien landscape to Leila. She realised she hadn't even missed it.

And she also realised that, in spite of her best intentions, she wasn't ready to say goodbye to Alix.

She nodded jerkily and said, 'Okay.'

The Place Vendôme was empty when they arrived, and they were escorted into the hotel with discreet efficiency. It gave Leila a bit of a jolt to see how the staff fawned over Alix, and how he instantly seemed to morph into someone more aloof, austere. She'd forgotten for a moment who he was.

When they entered his suite, low lamps were burning. Alix took off his jacket and Leila walked over to the window, feeling restless all of a sudden. She could see her shop, dark and empty, and a faint prickle of foreboding caused her to shiver minutely.

Then she saw Alix in the reflection of the window. He was looking at her. She turned around. The air shimmered between them. He came towards her and in a bid to break the intensity Leila glanced away, still a little overwhelmed by how much he made her *feel*.

And then something caught her eye on a nearby table, and when it registered she let out a gasp. 'Oh, *no!*'

Alix had spotted what Leila had spotted just a second afterwards and he cursed silently and vowed to have whoever had left the papers here sacked.

It was a popular French tabloid magazine and there was a picture on the front. A picture of Alix and Leila on a beach. They'd gone there the day before. They were sprawled in the sand, their swimwear leaving little to the imagination, but they were not naked, thankfully. Her face was turned away, up to his, so she wasn't identifiable— but he was.

Leila had already picked it up, but Alix whipped it out of her hands and threw it away. He said urgently, 'They didn't get your face…it's okay.'

She was pale, shocked. She looked up at him. 'You *knew* about this?'

Alix's conscience stung so much it hurt. Funny, he'd never considered himself to have much of a conscience. *Before.*

'My assistant sends me updates on any news coverage.'

Leila looked wounded. 'Why didn't you tell me?'

Alix gritted his jaw. 'Because I was hoping you wouldn't see it.'

Leila waved an arm. 'Well, the whole of France has seen it now.' She looked down to where the magazine was on the floor and read out, *'"Who is the exiled King's latest mystery flame?"'*

Alix caught her chin and moved it towards him. He felt her resistance. When she was looking at him he said, 'They don't know who you are and I'll make sure they won't. Please—trust me.'

Something moved across her face—some expression that Alix didn't like. Eventually she said, 'This has to end after tonight, Alix. I'm not made for your world and I don't want to be dragged through the papers as just another one of your women.'

Alix rejected everything she said, and a sense of desperation rose up inside him—that need to make her *his.* But he couldn't articulate it. So instead he used his mouth, moving it over hers, willing her to respond—and she did, because she was as helpless against this as he was.

The following morning when Leila woke up it took her a long time to orientate herself. She was in a massive bed, with the most luxurious coverings she'd ever felt. She was naked and alone. And her body ached. Between her legs she was tender.

And then it all flooded back. Alix had led her in here

last night and stripped her bare, as reverently as if she was something precious. Then he'd laid her down and subjected Leila to what could only be described as a sensual attack.

An attack that had been fully consensual.

It was as if everything he'd taught her had been only the first level, and his lovemaking last night had shown her that there could be so much more. Alix hadn't been tender or gentle. He'd been fierce, bordering on rough, but Leila blushed when she thought of how she'd revelled in it, meeting him every step of the way, exulting in it, spurring him on, raking her nails down his back, begging hoarsely for more, harder, deeper...

Even the fact that her picture had been in that magazine, albeit not identifiable, had faded into the background now.

She had a vague memory of finally falling asleep around dawn, with Alix's arms tight around her. Leila frowned as another memory struggled to break through her sluggish thought processes. Alix had kissed the back of her head and said, 'You're not going anywhere...this isn't over...'

Leila frowned. *Had* she heard that? And what could it mean? The prospect that Alix had decided that something more permanent might come out of what they had made her silly heart speed up.

She needed to talk to him.

Leila got out of bed and made her way to the opulent bathroom that her small apartment could have fitted into twice over. Once showered and dressed, she made her way to find Alix, hearing his low, deep tones before she saw him.

She smiled. Even his voice made heat curl in her belly as she recalled the way he sounded in bed—all earthy and husky and desperate... Maybe, just *maybe*, there was something different between them? The fact that she wasn't like his usual women—

Leila stopped in her tracks outside the door when she heard her name.

Alix spoke again. 'Leila's perfect, Andres. She's beautiful, accomplished, intelligent, refined.'

Leila blushed to find herself eavesdropping like this—and to hear herself being spoken of this way.

But Alix sounded a little angry when he spoke next. 'The very fact that she didn't want to be seen with me is a point in her favour. She's totally different to any other woman I've ever been with.'

Leila frowned minutely. *A point in her favour?* It sounded as if she was being graded.

She went to move forward, to let him know she was there, but when she got to the doorway she saw he was standing with his back to her, looking out of the window. So he didn't see her.

And when he spoke again his tone had the little hairs standing up on the back of her neck.

'To be perfectly honest,' he went on, 'I couldn't have possibly engineered this to go better if I'd planned it to happen. We're on the brink of a referendum that will return me to the throne and the ruling party haven't a clue. They probably think I'm still sunning myself with her on a beach in the Caribbean. Everything is falling into place at just the right time.'

Leila stepped back through the doorway, out of sight, horror coursing through her, her skin going clammy with shock.

Alix laughed and it was harsh. 'Since when has *love* had any relevance when it comes to the wife I will choose? The important thing is that she's falling in love with *me*—I'm

sure of it. This will be nothing like my parents' marriage…
toxic from the inside out.'

He continued, oblivious to the devastation taking place
just outside the door as the full import of what he was
saying sank into Leila.

'How do I know? She was a *virgin*, Andres…a woman
doesn't give that up easily. To return to power with a fiancée by my side will put me in a much stronger position. Leila will make a great queen, I'm sure of it. She's
the right choice.'

He was silent again, and then he spoke in a low voice.

'No, I've no doubt that she'll say yes. If I need to reassure her that I love her too, to achieve my aims, then
so be it. It won't be a hardship. And the sooner we have
children the better—an heir will be the strongest sign of
stability for Isle Saint Croix. A sign of hope and things
moving on.'

Leila's heart was pounding so hard she thought she
might faint. Sweat was breaking out on her brow.

*She was a virgin…a woman doesn't give that up eas-
ily. If I need to reassure her that I love her too…then
so be it.*

For a moment a sharp pain near her heart almost caused
her to double over. What Alix was proposing to do made
her feel sick. He would embark on a life with her based on
lies and falsehoods just so that he could present the whole
package to his precious island. An island that he was on
the brink of regaining after he'd let her believe that it was
a far distant possibility—not imminent. He'd lied to her
face! And he would father a child purely to further his
own political aims!

The irony was like a slap in the face—her own father
had rejected a child for the same reasons. But Leila was
in no mood to appreciate that dark humour now.

All their conversations took on a sinister glow now. His questions about her opinions on politics—had that been to make sure she wasn't some kind of raving anarchist? His questions on her opinions on anything had just been an interview.

And the intensity of their lovemaking—had that been to make sure Alix felt she could sustain his interest long enough for him to father an heir?

What broke her out of her shock was the fact that Alix had stopped talking. Feeling sick, Leila walked to the door, silent on the carpet. He was still standing at the window with his hands in his pockets. Master of all he surveyed—including, as he obviously believed, his innocent, gullible lover. A ruthless man who saw her only as a vehicle to help him regain his throne.

Leila felt the slow burn of an anger so intense it made her tremble. She only wanted one thing: to walk away from Alix and forget that she'd ever met him, forget that she'd repeated the sin of her mother: falling for the first man to seduce her.

Alix's brain was still whirring after the phone call. Had he really told Andres that he was prepared to make Leila his wife? His Queen?

Yes. He waited for a sense of regret, panic or claustrophobia. But even now it felt right. He'd never met anyone like her. She was sweet, innocent…and yet not so innocent any more. His body tightened as he recalled how quickly she'd learned, her shyly erotic, bold moves in bed, how she'd taken him in her mouth and tasted him a few short hours ago.

His body went still. A familiar figure walking quickly across the square came into his line of vision and his breath caught.

It was Leila, and she was carrying her holiday bag—the only woman he'd ever known not to travel with twelve pieces of luggage. Where was she going? His skin prickled uncomfortably when he recalled the phone conversation—was there a chance she'd overheard him?

But if she had why was she walking away? What woman would walk away from the prospect of a man like him making their union permanent?

A small voice whispered: *A woman like Leila.*

Alix was about to follow her when his phone rang again. He picked it up and said curtly, 'Yes?' He could see her now, disappearing into her shop, and he didn't like the flare of panic in his gut. The feeling that if he didn't follow her he'd never see her again.

'Your Majesty, are you there? We need to discuss plans for when the result of the referendum is announced tomorrow.'

Tomorrow. Tomorrow was when his life would change for ever. That reminder was a jolt to Alix. A jolt that told him he was in danger of losing focus when he needed it most. Over a woman. Even if she *was* the woman he'd chosen to be his Queen, she was still just a lover, a woman, peripheral to his life.

Alix pushed the insidious feeling of something slipping out of his grasp out of his head and concentrated on the call. For half an hour. When it was finally over he went to look out of the window again, and when he took in the view, every muscle in his body locked tight.

Leila was across the square, closing the door to her shop. The blinds were down and she was dressed in jeans, sneakers and a jacket. With a wheelie travel bag.

And as he watched she hitched up the handle on her bag and started to walk swiftly away from the shop, the bag trailing behind her.

* * *

Leila was almost at the corner of the street when Alix caught up with her, catching her arm. She didn't turn around and he felt the tension in her body.

'How much did you hear?' He directed the question to the back of her head.

She turned around then, and Alix steeled himself for some emotion, but Leila's face was expressionless in a way he'd never seen before. It sent something cold through him—along with a very uncomfortable sense of exposure.

'Enough. I heard enough, Alix.' She pulled her arm free and said, 'Now, if you'll excuse me, I have a train to catch.'

Alix frowned. Just a couple of hours ago he'd left her sated and flushed from their lovemaking in his bed. He'd whispered words to her—words he'd never thought he'd hear himself say to any woman. That sense of exposure amplified.

'Where are you going?'

Leila looked surprised. 'Oh, didn't I tell you? I've got to go to Grasse to discuss sharing new factory space with an old mentor of my mother's.'

Alix felt panic and he didn't like it. 'No, you didn't tell me.'

Leila looked at her watch. 'Well, I must have forgotten to mention it—'

She went to walk around him but he stopped her with a hand on her arm again. It felt slender under his hand.

Leila looked expressively at his hand. 'Let me go, please.'

'You had no plans to go anywhere until you overheard that conversation.'

Her eyes blazed into his. 'Don't you mean your royal decree?'

Alix was aware that they were drawing interest from

passers-by and he saw the glint of something in the distance that looked suspiciously like the lens of a paparazzi camera.

He gritted his jaw. 'We need to talk—and not in the street.'

Leila must have seen something on his face, because she looked mutinous for a second and then pulled her arm free again and started back towards her shop.

Alix took her case from her hand, although she held on to it until she obviously realised it would end up in a tug of war. She let him take it and the incongruity of the fact that he, Alix Saint Croix, was tussling over a case in the street with a woman was not lost on him.

When she'd opened the door to her shop they stepped inside and she shut it again. Alix fixed his gaze on her pale face. 'Why were you leaving?' *And without saying goodbye...* He bit back those words. Women didn't say goodbye to him—he said goodbye to *them*.

She folded her arms across her chest. She was mad at him—that much was patently obvious. 'I was leaving because I need to sort my business out. And also because your arrogance is truly astounding.' She unlocked her arms enough to point a finger at herself. 'How dare you assume that I'm falling in love with you? We've only known each other for two weeks. Or did you think that because I was a virgin I had less brain cells than the average woman and would fall for the first man I slept with?'

Alix felt something violent move through him at the implication that there would be more men and that he'd just been the first.

Now she looked even angrier. 'You told someone called Andres I was a virgin. How dare you discuss my private details with anyone else?'

Alix gritted his jaw harder. 'Unfortunately the life of

a royal tends to be public property. But it wasn't my right to divulge that information.'

Leila huffed a harsh-sounding laugh. 'Well, that's a life I have no intention of ever knowing anything about, so from now on I'd appreciate it if you kept details of our affair to yourself. You can rest assured, *Your Majesty*, I'm not falling in love with you.'

Alix told himself she wouldn't have run like that if something about overhearing that phone call hadn't affected her emotionally.

His eyes narrowed on her. 'So you say.'

'So I *mean*,' Leila shot back, terrified that he'd seen something else on her face. 'I've saved you the bother of having to pretend that you feel something for me, so I'll save you more time with the undoubtedly fake romantic proposal you had in mind...the answer is no.'

Alix lifted a brow. 'You'd say no to becoming a queen? And a life of unlimited wealth and luxury?'

Leila's stomach roiled. 'I'd say no to a marriage devoid of any real human emotion living in a gilded cage. How can you, of all people, honestly think I'd want to bring a child into the world to live with two parents who are acting out roles?'

Alix's eyes were steely. 'You weren't acting a role this morning.'

Immediately Leila was blasted with memory: her legs wrapped around Alix's waist, fingers digging into his muscular buttocks. What had she turned into? Someone unrecognisable.

She huffed a small unamused laugh. 'Surely you don't mean to confuse lust with love, Alix? I thought you were more sophisticated than that?'

His face flushed at that but it didn't comfort Leila. She felt nauseous.

'Look,' Alix said tersely, 'I know that you're probably a little hurt. The fact is that the woman I choose to be my Queen has to fulfil a certain amount of criteria. We respect each other. We like each other. We have insane chemistry. Those are all good foundations for a marriage. Better than something based on fickle emotions or antipathy from the start.'

Something dangerously like empathy pierced Leila when she thought of what he'd told her about his parents' marriage.

And then she thought of his assessment of her being a *little* hurt, and the empathy dissolved. The hurt was all-encompassing and totally humiliating. The last thing she wanted was for him to suspect for a second how devastating hearing that conversation had been.

'You never even told me you were so close to regaining your throne,' she accused.

Alix's jaw was hard as granite. 'I couldn't. Only my closest aides know of this.'

'So everything—the whole trip to your island—was all an elaborate attempt to throw your opponents off the scent? And what was I? A decorative piece for your charade? A convenient lover in the place of the last one you dumped so summarily?' Leila laughed harshly and started to pace. '*Mon Dieu*, but I was a fool, indeed. Two times in a row now.'

Alix sounded harsh. 'I am *not* like that man, and you were *not* a fool.'

Leila's gaze snapped back to his, but she barely saw him through her anger. 'Yes, I was. To have believed for a second that a trip like that was spontaneous.' She recalled something else about the conversation she'd overheard and gasped. '*You* had someone take those pictures of us, didn't you?'

Alix flushed. He didn't deny it.

Leila shook her head and backed away from him. The tender shoots of something that she'd been frantically trying to ignore finally withered away. She'd thought they'd been sharing intimate moments alone…he'd led her to believe they were alone on the island. She'd bared her body and soul to this man and he'd exploited that. She had to protect herself now.

She needed to drive him away before he saw how fragile she really was underneath her anger.

She affected nonchalance. 'To be perfectly honest, Alix, I used *you*.'

I used you. Alix reacted instantly, with an inward clenching of his gut. Pain.

An echo of the past whispered at him—another woman. *'I used you, Alix. I wanted back into Europe and I saw you as a means to get there and restore my reputation.'*

He went cold and hard inside. 'Used me?'

Leila nodded and shrugged lightly. 'I wanted to lose my virginity but I'd never met anyone with whom it was a palatable prospect…until you walked into the shop.'

Her eyes were like hard emeralds.

'It was only ever about that for me, Alix. And excitement—I won't deny that. My mother was overprotective, but now I'm finally free and independent, and I'm not about to shackle myself to some marriage of convenience because you deem me a suitable candidate for being your bride and the mother of your precious royal heirs.'

A mocking expression came over her face.

'I'm annoyed that you used me for your own ends, but that's the extent of any *hurt*. And surely you don't think you're the first rich man to invite me up to his suite for a private consultation?'

She didn't wait for a response.

'Well, you weren't the first, and you probably won't be the last.'

Alix's vision blurred for a moment at the thought of Leila going into another suite, smiling at some man, taking out her bottles. *Getting under his skin.* Concocting the perfect scent for him like a sorceress. Sleeping with him.

Darkness reared up inside him. She'd used him. Just as he'd been used before. He'd vowed never to let it happen again. Yet he had. The evidence of such weakness made him feel bilious. He'd been prepared to woo her into becoming his bride. He'd been prepared to take her into his life, parade her as his Queen. Prepared for her to bear his children. The heirs of Isle Saint Croix.

One thing broke through his mounting rage. 'You could be pregnant.'

The thought was repugnant to him now, when a couple of hours ago he'd thought it might be something used to persuade her to agree to marriage.

Leila went a little paler, but then her chin lifted. 'I'm not.'

Alix wanted there to be no doubt. None. 'How do you know?'

'I got my period this morning.'

Alix smiled humourlessly. 'And I suppose you'd have me believe that if you were pregnant you wouldn't come after me for everything you could?'

Alix was aware of her arms dropping and her hands fisting at her sides. *He* felt nothing, though. Only a desire to lash out.

'Your cynicism really knows no bounds. And now I have that train to catch. Please leave.'

Alix took a step back and forced himself to be civil when he wanted to swipe a hand across the nearest glittering shelf covered in glass bottles and bring them all crashing to the ground. To crush Leila under the burning anger in his gut, forcing her out of this hard obduracy. Force her to be soft and pliant again.

The desire made him feel disgusted with himself.

He turned and walked out of the shop.

It wasn't until Alix reached his suite in the hotel that his brain cleared of its dark haze.

He couldn't even accuse Leila of avariciousness. There were a million other women who would have heard that conversation and used it to inveigle their way into his life, take everything he offered and more. But not her.

The dark irony mocked Alix.

He saw the rumpled sheets on the bed out of the corner of his eye—and something else. He strode into his bedroom and picked up the House of Leila perfume bottle, containing his signature scent.

An image came to him of Leila in the bath, after they'd made love for the first time. He saw it as clearly as if she was in the room right now. The small sensual smile that had played around her mouth, her hand on her breast, a nipple trapped between her fingers. That smile scored his insides now like a knife. She'd looked *satisfied*. Mission accomplished. *I used you.*

Acting on a rising tide of rage, Alix lifted his arm and hurled the bottle at the nearest wall, where it smashed into a million tiny shards and scattered golden liquid everywhere. And that smell reached into his gut and clenched hard.

He lifted the phone and gave curt instructions that he and his entire team were to be moved to another hotel.

And just after that call he got another one from Andres. The man was excited.

'The polls are in and they're all suggesting a landslide victory. The government is panicking but it's too late. This is it, Alix. It's almost time to go home. When you return with Leila on your arm—'

Alix cut him off coldly. 'Do not mention her name again. Ever.'

There was silence on the other end of the phone before the man recovered with professional aplomb and went on as if nothing had happened.

Alix listened with a grim expression.

When the conversation was finished, staff appeared, scurrying to do his bidding. Alix cursed himself for over-reacting. Leila Verughese was just a woman. A beautiful woman. And it had been lust that had clouded his judgment. Just lust. Nothing more. If anything, it was a timely and valuable lesson.

By the time Alix was getting out of his car and entering his new temporary home, Leila Verughese wasn't a recent or even a distant memory. She had been excised from his mind with the kind of clinical precision Alix had used for years to excise anything he didn't want to think about. Women…the death of his brother.

His destiny was about to be resurrected from the ashes like a phoenix, and that was the most important thing in the world.

It was only when the train had left Paris far behind that Leila felt some of the rigid tension seep out of her locked muscles. Her jaw unclenched. The ache in her throat eased slightly.

She sent up silent thanks for the old friend of her mother's who would let her stay for a while with her in

Grasse. There was no meeting about sharing factory space, but it would get her out of Paris until Alix was gone.

And then the pain started to seep in from where she'd been blocking it out. The pain that told her it had taken more strength than she'd thought she had to stand in front of Alix and pretend he'd meant nothing to her. That she'd used him.

He'd used her. Thank God the press hadn't discovered her identity.

Her naivety made her want to be sick. And that reminded her of the slightly nauseous feeling she'd had for the last few days—not strong enough to cause concern, but there in the background. She'd put it down to Matilde's rich food.

She'd lied to him about her period. It hadn't come yet. But she'd wanted him gone. If he'd thought there was the slightest chance... Horror swept through her at the prospect.

She put her hand on her belly now and told herself fiercely that she *wouldn't* be pregnant, because the universe wouldn't be so cruel as to inflict the sins of the mother on the daughter. It couldn't.

If she *was* pregnant she didn't want to contemplate Alix Saint Croix's reaction. After their last conversation he would advocate only one thing to protect his precious ascent to power: termination. Because Leila Verughese had just comprehensively ruled herself out of the suitable bride stakes.

CHAPTER EIGHT

Seven weeks later

ALIX LOOKED OUT over the view from where his office was situated in the fortress castle of Isle Saint Croix. It was at the back, where the insurmountable wall of the castle dropped precipitously to the sea and the rocks below. The most secure room.

The window was open, allowing the mildly warm sea breeze to come in, bringing with it all the scents of his childhood that he'd never forgotten: earth, sea, wild flowers. And the more exotic scents of spices and herbs that always managed to infiltrate the air were coming from the main town's market.

It had been a tumultuous few weeks, to say the least, but he was still here and that was something.

Leila. She was a constant ghost in his mind. Haunting him. Tormenting him. As soon as he'd returned to Isle Saint Croix on a wave of triumph the perfume of the island had reminded him indelibly of her. Of the perfume she'd made for him.

Was she sitting in a luxurious hotel suite right now, with her potions arrayed before her? Smiling at some hapless man? Enthralling him? *Witch.*

He still couldn't believe she'd turned her back on the

opportunity to become his Queen. Or that her rejection had smarted so badly. He told himself it was a purely ego-based blow. He'd chosen Leila because he'd genuinely believed she had the necessary attributes. Plus he'd had the evidence that they got on well, and he'd felt she had integrity and that he could trust her.

Not to mention the insane chemistry between them.

And all along she'd had her own agenda.

An abrupt knock at the door interrupted his brooding and made him scowl. 'Come in.'

It was Andres, looking worried. Holding a tablet in his hand. When he got to Alix's desk he was grim. 'There's something you need to see.'

He turned the device around and Alix looked down to see rolling news footage. It took a second to compute what he was looking at, but when he did his entire body tensed and a wave of heat hit him in the solar plexus.

It was a picture of him and Leila, arguing in the street that day seven weeks ago. He had his hand on her arm and she looked angry. And beautiful. Even now it took his breath away.

The headline read: '*Want to meet the very fragrant mystery lover of the new King of Isle Saint Croix? Turn to page six...*'

Alix looked at Andres. 'Do it.'

Andres scrolled through and stopped. Alix read, but couldn't really take it in. Words jumped out at him:

Illegitimate secret daughter of Alain Bastineau... next President of France?
Pregnancy test...positive...royal heir?
Does King Alix know if he's the father?
Scandal and controversy don't seem to want to leave this new King in peace...

* * *

Leila was still in shock. It hadn't left her system yet even though she'd had since yesterday to come to terms with the news. She'd had it confirmed, after weeks of trying to deny the possibility when one period hadn't materialised and then the next one. She was pregnant—approximately eight weeks, according to the doctor she'd gone to see after doing three home tests: positive, positive, *positive*.

Pregnant and without the father. Just like her mother.

A sense of shame and futility washed over her. It was genetic. She'd proved no less susceptible to a gorgeous man intent on seduction. The only difference being that this time around the father would have been quite content to marry the mother of his child.

Leila smiled, but it was mirthless. Perhaps that was progress? Maybe by the next generation her child would manage *not* to get pregnant and would avoid dealing with the prospect of rejection and/or a convenient marriage?

Oh, God. Leila clutched her belly. Her child. A son or daughter. With this legacy in its past. How pathetic. Bitter tears made her eyes prickle.

A furious pounding on the door of the shop downstairs made her jerk suddenly upright. She heard a clamour of voices. She was late opening up, but her clientele hardly arrived in droves, so desperate to get into the shop that they'd pound on the door like that.

Momentarily distracted out of her circling thoughts, Leila hurried down to the shop, thinking that perhaps an accident had happened.

More banging on the door…urgent voices. Leila fumbled with the lock and swung the door wide—only to be met with a barrage of flashing lights, shouting voices and people pushing towards her.

It was so shocking and unexpected it took a moment for what they were saying to sink in, and then she heard it.

'Is it true you're pregnant with Alix Saint Croix's baby?'
'Are you getting back together?'
'How long have you been seeing him?'
'Why did you fight?'
'Are you in touch?'
'Does he know about the baby?'

The voices morphed into one and Leila finally had the presence of mind to slam the door shut again before someone got their foot in the door. Just before she closed it, though, someone threw in a newspaper and it landed at her feet.

She bent down to pick it up. Emblazoned across the front page was a picture of her and Alix arguing in the street that day all those weeks ago, his hand on her arm, her face tilted up to his: angry. *Hurt, humiliated.* She cringed now to see her emotions laid so bare. So much for believing she'd been in control.

And the headline: *'Leila Verughese, secret lover of Alix Saint Croix and the even more secret daughter that Alain Bastineau never wanted you to discover.'*

They knew about her father.

Leila's back hit the door and she slid down it as her legs turned to jelly. She barely noticed the pounding on the door, the shouting outside. She just knew that however bad she'd believed things to be just minutes before… when she'd known she was pregnant and it had still been her secret…they were about to get exponentially worse.

From somewhere came a persistent and non-stop buzzing noise. Leila dimly recognised that it was the phone. On hands and knees she crawled over to where the device sat under the counter. She picked it up.

Somehow she wasn't surprised to hear the familiar authoritative male voice. It caused her no emotion, though. She was numb with shock.

It told her that in one hour Ricardo would be at the back lane entrance of her property with a decoy. She was to let him in. In the meantime she was to pack a bag, and then leave with him when instructed.

The shock kept Leila cocooned from thinking too much about these instructions, or the baying mob outside. And in just over an hour she let Ricardo in, with a girl who looked disconcertingly like her... Leila didn't think twice about letting them borrow one of her coats for the girl, nor about the fact that he sent the girl out through the front. The baying mob reached fever pitch and then suddenly died down again as she heard vague shouts of, *'She's getting away!'*

Ricardo was saying urgently, 'It won't be long, Miss Verughese, before they realise she's not you. Where is your bag? We need to lock up and go—now.'

And then Leila was being escorted into the back of a car with blackened windows and they were racing through the streets of Paris. At one point Ricardo must have been concerned by her shocked compliance and pallor as he asked if she was okay. She caught his eye in the mirror and said numbly, 'Yes, thank you, Ricardo.'

The shock finally started dissipating when they pulled up outside one of Paris's most iconic and exclusive hotels. It seemed as if a veritable swarm of black-suited men appeared around the car, and one of them was opening her door.

Leila looked at Ricardo, who'd turned around to face her.

'It's okay, Miss Verughese, they're the King's security staff. They have instructions to bring you straight to him.'

The King. He was a king now. Leila blanched. 'He's here?'

Ricardo nodded. 'He flew in straight away. He's waiting for you.'

The man almost looked sympathetic now, and that galvanised Leila. No way was she going to be made to feel that she was in the wrong here. Her life had just been torn to pieces and it was all *his* fault.

The wave of righteous indignation lasted until she was standing outside imposing doors on one of the top floors of the luxurious hotel and the bodyguard escorting her was knocking on the polished wood.

Indignation was fast being replaced with nerves and trepidation and nausea. *She was going to see him again.*

She wanted to turn and run. She wasn't ready—

A voice came from inside the suite, deep and cold and imperious. 'Come.'

The bodyguard opened the door with a card and ushered her in. Leila all but fell over the threshold to find herself in a marbled lobby that would have put a town house to shame.

It was circular, and doors led off in various directions. For a second she wanted to giggle. She felt like Alice in Wonderland.

And then a tall, broad shape darkened one of the doorways. *Alix.* He looked even bigger than before, dressed in a three-piece suit. His hair was severely short and he was clean shaven. Leila immediately felt weak and hated herself for it.

She fought it back and lifted her chin. 'You summoned me, Your Majesty?'

Alix's face darkened. A muscle pulsed in his jaw. He didn't rise to her bait, though, just stood aside and said, 'We need to talk—please come in.'

Leila moved forward and swept past him with all the confidence she could muster, quickly moving into the enormous room with its huge windows looking out over the Place de la Concorde, with the Eiffel Tower just visible in the distance.

She'd tried not to breathe his scent as she passed, but it was futile. She found herself drinking it in…it seemed to cling to her…but she couldn't find any of the notes she'd made for him. It was the scent he'd had *before*. She felt a pang of hurt. He wasn't wearing her scent any more…

She looked out of the window and folded her arms over her chest, wishing she felt more presentable. Wishing she wasn't wearing the same old dark trousers, white shirt, flat shoes. Hair up in a neat ponytail for work. No make-up.

'Is it true? Are you pregnant?'

Leila fought the urge to bring a hand down to cover her belly protectively, as if she could protect the foetus from hearing this conversation.

'Yes, it's true,' she said tightly.

'And it's mine?'

She sucked in a breath and turned around. 'Of course it's yours—how dare you imply—?'

Alix held up a hand. He looked cold and remote. She'd never seen him like this apart from at that last meeting.

'I *imply* because *I* come with quite a considerable dowry.'

Leila bit out, 'Well, if you remember, you have come to me—not the other way around.'

Alix dug his hands into his pockets. 'And would you have come to me?'

Leila opened her mouth and shut it again, a little blindsided. But she knew that her fear of how Alix would have reacted would have inhibited her from telling him—at least straight away.

She avoided answering directly. 'I've only just found out for sure. I haven't had much time to take it in myself.'

That was the truth.

Alix looked so obdurate right then that it sent a prickle of fear down Leila's spine. 'I'm not getting rid of it just because I'm not suitable wife material any more.'

He frowned. 'Who said anything about getting rid of it?' His frown deepened and then an expression came over his face—something like disgust. 'You suspected you might be pregnant that day, didn't you?'

Leila's face got hot. She glanced down at the floor, feeling guilty. 'I *hadn't* got my period.' She looked up again. 'But I didn't want to say anything. I had no reason to believe it wasn't just late, and I was hoping that...' She stopped.

'That there would be no consequences?' Alix filled in, with a twist to his mouth.

Leila nodded.

'Well, there are. And rather far-reaching ones.'

More than fear trickled down her spine now. But before she could ask him to clarify what he meant he moved towards her. He stopped—too close. She could smell him, imagined she could feel his heat. She wanted to step back, but wouldn't.

'You lied to me.'

Leila frowned. 'But I only just found—'

'About your father. You said he was dead.'

Leila felt weak again. She'd conveniently let that little time bomb slide to the back of her head while dealing with this.

She glared at Alix. 'You lied too. You lied about the fact that you were poised to take control of your throne again and just using me as a smokescreen.'

Alix appeared to choose to ignore that. He folded his

arms. Eyes narrowed on her. 'Why did you lie about your father?'

Leila turned away from him again, feeling like a pinned insect under his judgemental gaze. He came alongside her. She bit her lip. He was silent, waiting.

Reluctantly she said, 'It was my mother. It was what she always said. *"He's dead to us, Leila. He didn't want me or you. And he only wanted me to prostitute myself for him. If anyone asks, he's dead."'*

Alix stayed silent.

'I was aware of who he was—his perfect life and family. His rise to political fame. Why would I ever admit that he was my father? I was ashamed for him. And for myself. It's one thing to be rejected by a parent who has known you all your life, but another to be rejected before they've even met you.'

She and her mother had seen both sides of that coin.

Alix's tone was arctic, he oozed disapproval of her messy past. 'We found out that the press sat on the story of your identity in order to dig into your past and see if they could find anything juicy. And they did. Your father is already doing his best to limit the damage, claiming these reports are spurious—an attempt to thwart his chances in the election.'

Leila hated it, but she felt hurt. Another rejection—and public this time. 'I'm not surprised,' she said dully. And in front of Alix. Could this day get any worse?

Apparently it could. From beside her he said briskly, 'The press conference will be taking place in an hour's time. I've arranged for a stylist and her team to come and get you ready.'

Leila turned to look at Alix. 'Press conference? Stylist? What for?'

Alix turned to face her. His expression brooked no

argument. 'A press conference to announce our engagement, Leila. After which you'll be leaving with me to come back to Isle Saint Croix.'

For some reason Leila seized on the most innocuous word. 'Back? But I've never been...' Her brain felt sluggish, words too unwieldy to say.

A sharp pinging noise came out of nowhere and Alix extracted a sleek phone from his pocket, holding it up to his ear. He took it away momentarily to say to Leila, 'Wait here for the stylist. I'll be back shortly.'

And he was walking out of the room before she could react.

When she did react, Leila felt red-hot lava flow through her veins. The sheer arrogance of the man! To assume she'd meekly roll over and agree to his bidding just because he had a King Kong complex!

Leila stormed off after Alix, going down seemingly endless corridors that ended in various plush bedrooms and sitting rooms, and a dining room that looked as if it could seat a hundred.

She eventually heard low voices from behind a closed door and without knocking threw the door open. 'Now, look here—what part of *I don't want to marry you* didn't you understand the first time I said it?'

Leila came to an abrupt halt when about a dozen faces turned to look at her. There were two women in the group, scarily coiffed and besuited. Alix was in the middle, looking stern, and they were all watching something on the television.

A man around Alix's age detached himself from the group and came over to Leila, holding out a hand. 'Miss Verughese—a pleasure to meet you. I'm Andres Balsak, King Alix's chief of staff.'

Leila let him take her hand, feeling completely exposed.

Andres let her hand go and urged her in with a hand on her elbow. 'We're watching a news report.'

The crowd parted and Leila was aware of their intense scrutiny. She avoided looking at Alix's no doubt furious expression.

The news report was featuring a very pretty town full of brightly coloured houses near a busy harbour. An imposing castle stood on a lushly wooded hill behind the town.

A reporter was saying, 'Will King Alix be able to weather this scandalous storm so early into his reign? We will just have to wait and see. Back to you—'

The TV was shut off. Alix said, 'Everyone out. *Now*.'

The room cleared quickly.

The reality of seeing that report, as short as it had been, brought home to Leila the stark magnitude of what she was facing.

She turned to Alix. 'What exactly is it that you're proposing with this press conference and by bringing me to Isle Saint Croix?'

Alix looked at Leila. She could have passed for eighteen. She was pale and even more beautiful than he remembered. Had her eyes always been that big? The moment he'd seen her standing in the foyer, his blood had leapt as if injected by currents of pure electricity.

And when she'd passed him, her scent had reminded him of too much. How easily he'd let her in. How much he still wanted her. How much he'd trusted her. Would she even have come to him to let him know about the baby? He had a feeling that she wouldn't, and his blood boiled.

Damn her. And damn that sense of protectiveness he'd

felt when she'd revealed the truth about her father. He couldn't think of that now.

'You'll come because you're carrying my heir and the whole world knows it now.'

Leila looked hunted, her arms crossed tightly over her chest again, pushing the swells of those luscious breasts up. They looked bigger. Because of the pregnancy? The thought of Leila's body ripening with his seed, his child, gave him another shockingly sudden jolt of lust. A memory blasted—of taking a nipple into his mouth, rolling it with his tongue, tasting her sharp sweetness—he brutally clamped down on the image.

Leila was pacing now. 'What is the solution here? There *has* to be a solution...' She stopped and faced him again. 'I mean, it's not as if you're *really* intending to marry me. The engagement is just for show, until things die down again...'

She looked so hopeful Alix almost felt sorry for her. *Almost.* Her reluctance to marry him caught at him somewhere very primal and possessive.

'No, Leila. We *will* be getting married. In two weeks. It's traditional in Isle Saint Croix to have short engagements.'

Leila squeaked, 'Two weeks?' She found a chair and sat down heavily. She looked bewildered. 'But that's ridiculous!'

Alix shook his head. 'It's fate, Leila. Our fate and our baby's. The child you're carrying is destined to be the future King or Queen of Isle Saint Croix. It will have a huge legacy behind it and ahead of it. Would you deny it that?'

Leila's arms uncrossed and her hands went to her lap, twisting. Alix had to stop himself from going over and lacing his fingers through hers.

'Well, of course not—but surely there's a way—?'

'And would you deny it the chance to grow up knowing its father? Surrounded by the security of a stable marriage? You of all people?'

Leila paled and stood up again. 'That's a low blow.'

Alix pressed on, ignoring the pang of his conscience *again*: 'We have a child to think of now. Our concerns are secondary. If you choose to go against me on this I will not hesitate to use my full influence to make you comply.'

'You bast—'

Alix spoke over her. 'There's not only our child to consider, but the people of Isle Saint Croix. Things have been precarious, to say the least, since I won back the throne. We are at a very delicate stage, and we desperately need to achieve stability and start getting the country back on its feet. Everything could descend into chaos again at a moment's notice. This scandal is all my enemies need to tip the balance. Would you allow that to be on your conscience?'

Leila thought of the pictures she'd just seen on the TV of the pretty town, the idyllic-looking island.

She swallowed. 'That's not fair, Alix. I'm not responsible for what happens to your people.'

'No,' he agreed. 'But I am, and I'm taking full responsibility for *this* situation.'

In the end it was the weight of inevitability and responsibility that got to Leila. And the realisation that she'd suspected all along that this might happen. Either this or Alix would have asked her to get rid of the baby. And the fact that he hadn't...

She put her hand over her belly now, that newly familiar sense of protectiveness rising up. She'd felt it as soon as the doctor had confirmed her pregnancy beyond all question. Along with a welling of helpless love. So this

was what her mother had gone through... It put a whole
new perspective on her mother, and how brave she'd been
to go it alone.

And Leila wasn't even facing that. She was facing
the opposite—a forced marriage to someone who pretty
much despised her after she'd told him she'd used him.
In a pathetic attempt to save face, to hide how hurt she'd
been.

And now she'd have to live with that. But as long as
she remembered Alix's phone conversation she wouldn't
lose her way. He'd never intended this to be anything but
a means to an end. And at least he hadn't fooled her into
thinking he'd fallen for her.

Her child would not suffer from the lack of a father as
she had done. Feeling rejected. Abandoned. Unwanted.
Alix might want this baby purely for what it represented:
continuity. But it would be up to Leila to make sure it
never, ever knew how ruthless its father was.

'There, Miss Verughese, see what you think.'

Leila smiled absently at the stylist who'd been waiting
with a rail of clothes when Alix had escorted her back
through the suite like a recalcitrant child. Someone had
also been there to do her hair and make-up.

She looked in the mirror now and sucked in a breath.
She looked totally different. Elegant. She wore a fitted
long-sleeved dress in soft, silky material. It was a deep
green colour, almost dark enough to be blue. It was mod-
est, in that it covered her chest to her throat, but it clung
in such a way that made it not boring. It fell from her hips
into an A-line shape, down to her knees.

Her hair was up in a chignon, showing off her neck.
Her eyes and cheekbones seemed to stand out even more.
She put it down to the artful make-up, and not the fact
that her appetite had waned in the last month.

She was given a pair of matching high heels. And then Alix appeared. He'd changed suits and was now wearing one with a tie that had colours reflecting those in Leila's dress. She reeled at the speed with which he'd reacted to the news and been prepared.

'Please leave us.'

Once again the room emptied as if by magic. Alix's cool grey gaze skated over Leila and she felt self-conscious. This man was a stranger to her. But a stranger who made her body thrum with awareness.

He held out a velvet box and opened it. Inside was a beautiful pair of dangling emerald and gold earrings. Ornate—almost Indian in their design.

She looked from them to him. 'They're beautiful.'

Alix said, 'They're part of the Crown Jewels. They were protected by loyalists to the crown while I was in exile. Put them on.'

Leila glared at him.

'Please,' he said.

She lifted them out, one by one, and put them on, feeling their heavy weight dangling near her jaw.

'I have something else…'

Alix was holding out a smaller velvet box. Her heart thumped hard. She'd dreamed of this moment, even though she'd never have admitted it to herself—but not like this. Not with waves of resentment being directed at her.

Alix opened it and she almost felt dizzy for a moment. Inside was the most beautiful ring she'd ever seen.

Five emeralds—clearly very old. Set in a dark gold ring. It was slightly uneven, imperfect.

Leila reached out a finger and touched it reverently. 'How old is this?'

Carelessly Alix said, 'Around mid-seventeenth century.'

She looked at him, horrified. 'I can't accept this.'

Alix sounded curt. 'It matches your eyes.'

Something traitorous moved inside her to think of him choosing jewellery because it matched her eyes. That he'd thought about it rather than just picking the first ring he saw.

Alix took the ring out of the box and took up Leila's left hand.

Immediately her body reacted and she tensed. Alix shot her a look before sliding the ring onto her ring finger and Leila held her breath. It was as if the fates and the entire universe were conspiring against her, because it fitted her perfectly.

Alix's hand was very dark next to her paler one, his fingers long and masculine. Hers looked tiny in comparison.

He didn't let her go and she looked up, confused.

Alix's expression was unreadable. 'There's one more thing.'

'More jewellery? I really don't need—'

But her words were cut off when Alix's head lowered and his mouth slanted over hers. She was so shocked she didn't react for a second, and that gave Alix the opportunity to coax open her mouth and deepen the kiss.

When Leila recovered her wits she tried to pull away, but Alix had a hand at the back of her head and stopped her from retreating. Everything sane in Leila was screaming at her to push him away, but her body was exulting in the kiss, drinking him in as if she'd been starved in a desert for weeks and had just found life-restoring water.

His scent intoxicated her, and before Leila could stop herself she was clutching at Alix's jacket and pressing her body closer to his.

A sharp rap at the door broke through the fog and Alix

broke contact. Leila didn't have time to curse him or herself, because Andres was popping his head around the door and saying, 'They're ready for you.'

Alix said abruptly, 'We'll be right there.'

Andres disappeared and Leila realised she was still clinging onto Alix's jacket. He was barely touching her. She took a step back. He was looking at her almost warily, as if she might explode. And she *had* almost exploded—in his arms. It was galling.

'What was that in aid of?' Her tongue felt too large for her mouth.

'The world's press are waiting for us downstairs. We need to convince them that this was a lovers' tiff and we are now happily reunited. That the pregnancy is the happy catalyst that has brought us back together.'

The speed and equanimity with which Alix seemed to be reacting to this whole situation, not to mention his attention to detail—*that kiss*—just confirmed for Leila how ruthless he was. And how she'd never really known him.

She wanted to kick off her heels and run as fast as she could for as long as she could. But she couldn't. Together they had created a baby, and that baby had to come first. Exactly as Alix had said.

She smoothed clammy hands down her dress and drew her shoulders straight. 'Very well—we shouldn't keep them waiting, then, should we?'

Alix watched Leila walk to the door and open it. Her spine was as straight as a dancer's and her bearing was more innately regal than any blue-blooded princess he'd ever met. Something like admiration mounted inside him, cutting through the eddying swirl of lust that still held his body in a state of heightened awareness and uncomfortable arousal.

He'd tried to block out the effect she had on him, telling himself it couldn't possibly have been as intense as he'd thought. But it had been *more*.

CHAPTER NINE

THE PLANE THAT was taking them to Isle Saint Croix was bigger than the plane Alix had used before. The fact that Leila had only ever travelled on private jets was something she should have found ironically amusing, but she couldn't drum up much of a sense of lightness now.

The press conference had passed in a blur of shouted questions and popping cameras. Leila had just about managed to lock her legs in place so they hadn't wobbled in front of everyone.

Andres had sent someone to retrieve her most important and portable possessions from her apartment and they were in a trunk in the hold.

Alix's staff, whom she'd seen in the suite in Paris, were all down at the back of the plane now, including Andres, and she and Alix were alone in the luxurious front. There was a sitting room, dining room and bedroom with en-suite bathroom. Stewards had offered dinner, but Leila had only been able to pick at it. Her stomach was too tied up in knots.

She thought of how Alix had responded to a question about her father at the press conference.

He'd said curtly, 'If Alain Bastineau is so certain he is not my fiancée's father, then let him prove it with a DNA test.'

Huskily Leila said now, 'When they asked about my father…you didn't need to respond like that.'

Alix looked at her. 'Yes, I did. Any man who rejects his own child is not a man. You're to be the Queen of Isle Saint Croix and I will not allow you to be speculated about in that way.'

Immediately Leila felt deflated. He'd only stood up for her because of concerns for his own reputation. She'd been stupid to see anything else in it, however tenuous.

'You need to eat more—you've lost weight.'

Alix was looking at her intently and Leila cursed herself for having drawn his attention. She felt defensive and, worse, self-conscious.

'Apparently it's common to lose weight when you're first pregnant.'

Alix's voice was gruff. 'We'll arrange for you to see the royal doctor as soon as you're settled. We need to organise your prenatal care.'

Leila was surprised at the vehemence in Alix's voice and had to figure that all this meant so much more to him than the fact of a baby. She and the baby now represented stability for the island's future.

She frowned then, thinking of something else. 'How did they find out?'

Alix was grim. 'I told you—they had that picture of us in the street and they sat on it, wanting to know more about you. Also, as I had just been crowned King again, they knew there was potentially a much bigger story in the offing. They were keeping an eye on you, Leila. We think someone went through your bins and found the home pregnancy tests you did.'

Leila instantly felt nauseous and put a hand to her mouth. She shot up out of her chair and made it to the bathroom in time to be sick. She knew it wasn't necessarily what Alix had just said—her bouts of nausea hit her at different moments of the night and day.

To her embarrassment, when she straightened up in the small bathroom she saw Alix reflected in the mirror, looking concerned. No doubt concerned for her cargo.

Weakly she said, 'I'm fine—it's normal.'

'You look as pale as a ghost. Lie down and rest, Leila. You'll need it.'

Alix went out into the bedroom and pulled back the covers. Leila kicked off her shoes and avoided his eye as she sat down. Then she thought of something else and looked up at him, panicked. 'What about my shop?'

Alix was grim. 'We can arrange for someone to manage it in the short term. It'll probably be for the best if you sell it. You'll be busy with your duties as Queen and as a mother.'

Furious anger raced through Leila's blood, galvanising her to stand, all weariness gone. 'How dare you presume to take my livelihood away from me just like that?' She snapped her fingers.

'Leila, look—'

'No, *you* look.' Leila stabbed a finger towards Alix, the full tumult of the day catching up with her. 'That business is my own family legacy. It's a vocation, making perfumes, and I will *not* be giving it up. If you insist otherwise then I won't hesitate to leave Isle Saint Croix on the first return flight out.'

She folded her arms tight across her chest.

'Or are you telling me that you'll incarcerate me like some feudal overlord? I'm sure the tabloids would love to hear about *that*!'

Alix's mouth was a thin line, and a muscle jumped in his jaw. Finally he said, 'Fine. We'll discuss how you can incorporate it into your life.'

And just as suddenly as the anger had come, it faded away, leaving her bone-weary again. Leila sat down on the side of the bed. Alix stood in her vision, huge and immovable.

Leila lay down and curled away from where he stood, eyes shut tight. Maybe when she woke up this would all be a bad dream...?

Alix stood looking down at the woman on the bed, seeing how her breath evened out and her muscles grew slacker. Her back was to him and that only compounded the frustration still rushing through his system. He knew he'd been out of line to suggest that Leila sell her business, but he found it hard not to operate from some base place when she was in front of him.

He'd noticed the minutely perceptible thickening of her waist. Her hand had rested there just now, as if to protect the child within. And suddenly an almost dizzying sense of protectiveness rose up within him.

He thought of those paparazzi hounding Leila, and recalled that when Andres had shown him the news footage, his primary instinct had been to get to her and keep her safe more than to confront her about the pregnancy.

It made him feel exposed.

Alix finally backed away from the bed and out of the room. When he sat down again he asked for a shot of whisky from the hovering attendant.

He swirled the dark amber liquid in the heavy crystal glass for a long moment. He'd always thought that having a child would be something he'd feel quite clinical about. Not entirely unemotional, of course. He would be as loving as he could be. But how could he be something he knew nothing of? A loving parent?

Alix had only ever really loved one person: his brother.

And the pain he'd felt when his brother had been murdered had nearly killed him too. He would never forget that raw chasm of rage and grief. And he never wanted to feel it again.

Except now his gut was churning with dark emotions that felt far too close to the bone.

When he'd first contemplated making Leila his Queen it had felt like a relatively uncomplicated decision. He liked her. Liked talking to her, spending time with her. Liked that he'd been her first lover. *Just* that memory alone was enough to have Alix's body hardening.

His mouth twisted. Their intense mutual chemistry had told him that there would be no issues in the bedroom.

For someone who had always known that his choice of bride would be strategic above all else, it had felt like a very logical choice. A beautiful bride…a queen he would have no hardship creating a family with.

Until she'd rejected his offer outright.

And now she was pregnant with his child and he had no choice but to make her his wife. He was being mocked by the gods for his initial complacency.

Alix willed down the heat in his body and the darkness in his gut. He'd believed that Leila was falling for him when evidently she hadn't been.

He ignored the intensifying of the tightness in his chest and told himself that this would only make things easier. No emotion on either side. No illusions. This was about the baby and the future of Isle Saint Croix, and while Leila was not the bride Alix would choose if he had a choice right now, he *would* make this work. For the sake of his people and for the sake of his legacy into the future.

When they arrived in Isle Saint Croix it was after midnight. Too late for any kind of formal reception, much to

Leila's relief. She was still feeling a little hollowed out and overwhelmed. Her sleep on the plane had been populated with scary dreams of her running and a tall, menacing figure trying to catch her. She didn't have to be a genius to figure that one out.

Her first impressions of the island were of warm, damp heat. Warmer than she'd expected. Stars populated the clear night sky. There was the zesty sea-salt freshness of the ocean nearby. And something much more exotic and intriguing.

On the journey to the castle Leila caught glimpses of small pretty villages and a bigger town down near the sea, lights twinkling in the harbour. Then they rounded a bend, and there on a hilltop in the distance stood the floodlit castle.

She couldn't hold in a gasp of pure awe. On the TV it had looked like a toy...now she could see just how massive and imposing it was. As if it had been hewn directly out of the rock of the mountainside.

Its influence was clearly Moorish, with its flat roofs and long walls and what looked like lots of quadrangular buildings. Something about it called to Leila—something in its stark beauty.

'That's the castle. Our home.'

Our home. It was surreal. Leila felt overwhelmed again and said, 'I don't even know what language you speak...'

Alix turned his head. 'It's a colloquial mixture of Spanish and French and Arabic. But the official language is French, thanks to the fact that the French were our longest colonisers until the mid-eighteenth century.'

'There's so much I don't know.'

'I'll arrange for Andres to find a tutor for you.'

The car was descending now, down winding steep roads into a sort of valley. Leila could see the lights of a town nearby—presumably the capital. And then they were bypassing it and climbing again, up towards the castle, in through ornate gates and up a long driveway.

When they arrived in a huge stone courtyard with a bubbling fountain in the centre the car drew to a stop. Leila could see through the tinted windows to where a large handsome woman was waiting for them.

When they were out of the vehicle Alix led Leila over to her and said, with evident fondness in his voice, 'This is Marie-Louise, the castle manager. She and her husband risked their lives to protect some of my family's oldest artefacts, including the Crown Jewels.'

Leila's engagement ring winked at her in the moonlit night. 'That was very brave of you.'

The woman beamed and then ushered them inside to where the castle spread out into what seemed to be a warren of imposing stone corridors and inner courtyards.

Alix spoke to the woman in his own seductive tongue. He was obviously telling her goodnight, because she walked away from them.

He let Leila's hand go and indicated for her to precede him down a long corridor. It was lit by small flaming lanterns and for a moment Leila had the sensation that they might have slipped back in time and nothing would have changed.

They were approaching a wall that held a huge wooden door, ornately carved. The guard there stood aside and bowed as Alix opened the door and led them through.

'These are the royal family's private apartments.' He stopped outside another door and opened it. 'And these are your rooms.'

Leila felt a kind of giddy relief mixed with disappointment. She looked at Alix. 'We won't have to share a room?'

Alix saw that vaguely hopeful look on Leila's face and it made him feel rebellious. He desisted from telling her that his own parents had not shared rooms. That it would be considered perfectly normal if they had their own suites.

He shook his head. 'This is just until we're married—to observe propriety.'

Leila's hopeful look faded and became something else—something cynical, hunted. She gestured to her belly. 'It's not as if people don't *know* we've already consummated our relationship.'

Alix had to battle the urge to remind her of just what that consummation had felt like. The magnitude of the fact that Leila was here under his roof, pregnant, was hitting him in a very deep and secret place.

He ruthlessly pushed it down and walked into the suite. 'I hope you'll find the apartment comfortable.'

Leila had followed him in and was looking around with big eyes. He saw it as if for the first time again: the understated luxury that the ruling regime had seen fit to keep for themselves. It was a little shabby now, but still with shades of its former opulent glory.

A glory that would be fully restored.

With his wife by his side.

With that in mind Alix forced out all emotion and said, 'The sleeping quarters are accessed back through the main hall. I have instructed that you are to have everything you might need.'

Leila looked at him and he could see the faint shadows under her eyes. Like delicate bruises.

The fact that she didn't want to be here sat like a dense heavy stone in his chest. He ignored it. She wouldn't have that power over him.

'I've made an arrangement for a scan at the hospital tomorrow—apparently you're due one about now.'

Leila's mouth twisted. 'To check on the cargo? Make sure that it's all looking good before you commit?'

Alix gritted his jaw at the sudden urge he had to go over and slam his mouth down on hers, making those mutinous lines soften.

'Something like that.' He moved towards the door. 'You should rest, Leila. The next few days will be busy.'

And then he left, almost afraid that she'd see something of the lack of control he felt.

Leila watched Alix leave. She was barely aware of the beauty of her surroundings, only vaguely aware that they'd walked through an open-air courtyard to come into the living room.

She felt numb with tiredness, delayed shock and the lingering effects of adrenaline.

Exploring back through the main hall, she found a bathroom off the bedroom. It was massive, with a grand central sunken tub. The dressing room was a more modern room, luxuriously carpeted and filled from floor to ceiling with clothes. A central island held hundreds of accessories in various shelves and drawers—and underwear. Underwear that made her cheeks grow hot.

She hurriedly shut those drawers, knowing how wasted the lovely underwear would be—because clearly Alix felt no desire for her any more, despite that kiss earlier, which had just been for appearances. He'd looked at her since as if he could hardly bear to be in the same room as her.

She ignored the pain near her heart and found the least skimpy nightwear she could find. Silk pyjamas. After conducting a rudimentary toilette and carefully putting the jewellery away in a drawer, she climbed into a bed that might have slept a football team and tried not to be too intimidated by the grandeur.

For a long time she looked up at the ceiling. Leila couldn't stop thinking about the fact that if Alix didn't desire her any more, then what glue could possibly hold their union together beyond duty and a shared responsibility for their child?

The following early afternoon Leila was pacing in the sitting room of her lavish suite. Marie-Louise had appeared that morning with a meek-looking girl who apparently was to be Leila's personal maid. When Leila had protested she'd been ignored and all but marched into a small dining room, where a delicious breakfast had been laid out. Her stomach had still been in knots, so she hadn't eaten much.

She'd explored thoroughly now, and had discovered the beautiful open-air atrium had a small pool, with glittering mosaics on the bottom and brightly coloured fish darting back and forth.

There was also a terrace outside her bedroom doors, and a balcony that overlooked the town far below with its brightly painted houses and the harbour.

Smells had tickled her nostrils, making her tip her head back to breathe deep. Earth, flowers, the sea, a distant wood... And then she'd realised why Alix had reacted so strongly to the scent she'd made. She'd somehow managed intuitively to recreate the scents of this island without having ever been there before.

Hating it that she felt so hurt because he obviously didn't wear the scent any more, Leila focused on checking herself in a nearby mirror. She'd had to pick a dress from the vast array of clothes in the dressing room as her own clothes hadn't appeared yet. She'd chosen a simple wrap dress in a very deep blue, and matching shoes.

She plucked at the material now, feeling that it was gaping over her breasts, which were sensitive and felt inordinately swollen.

She put a hand on her belly, knowing that it hadn't grown perceptibly in size, but feeling a telltale bloatedness.

'How are you today?'

Leila jumped and whirled around to see Alix behind her, hands in his pockets, dressed in a simple dark suit and white shirt. Every inch of him exuded pure masculine power and sensuality. And that new reserve tinged with disapproval.

The carpet must have muffled his steps. She hated it that he'd caught her in a private moment like that. And that her body had immediately zapped to life in his presence, nerve endings tingling.

She lifted her chin. 'Time to confirm all is well with your precious heir?'

His eyes glittered, as if he was angry at her insolence. 'The doctor is waiting for us at the hospital.'

Alix stood back to let Leila precede him from the room and she prayed he wouldn't see how brittle her sense of control was.

They walked down another seemingly unending labyrinth of imposing stone corridors and Leila had much more of a sense of the grandeur of the castle. She had to admit it: she was *impressed*. It was a little overwhelming, to say the least.

As was the display when they got to the entrance of the castle and about a dozen bodyguards jumped to attention. Alix opened the passenger door of a Jeep for Leila and after she was in got in the driver's side.

She watched him take the wheel with easy confidence, the guards preceding them and following them.

Slightly nervously, Leila asked, 'You said things were precarious here—is there any danger?'

Alix flashed her a look and she saw his jaw tighten before he said, 'I would never put you or the baby in danger. We are being protected by the best security firm in the world.'

Leila was slightly taken aback at his vehemence and said, 'I didn't mean to imply that you'd put me—*us*—in danger.' She'd realised, of course, that Alix probably couldn't care less if she was in danger. It was the baby he cared about.

She saw his hands tighten on the wheel and then relax. 'Forgive me. But you don't have to worry. The opponents to the throne are small in number, and weakened after years of not living up to their promises to build an egalitarian society. They have no real power. I've made sure of that. Still, I would never take anything for granted—hence the protection until Isle Saint Croix is on a much more solid footing economically.'

They were driving through the town now, and Leila could see its charm up close. She could also see that it was badly in need of sprucing up, with a general sense of neglect pervading the air.

A few people waved at their Jeep and Alix waved back. He said now, 'It's going to take time for the people to adjust to having their King back. They're not sure how to deal with me yet.'

Leila asked, with a feeling of something like disappointment, 'And do you really want them bowing and scraping to you?'

Alix looked at her again, slightly incredulous. 'God, *no*. I couldn't imagine anything worse.'

He looked back to the road, one hand on the wheel, the other on his thigh. Which Leila found very distracting, as she remembered how those thighs had pushed hers apart so that he could sink deep—

'I want to live side by side with my people. To move among them as an equal. I don't want pomp and ceremony. But equally I want to be their leader and protector. To provide for them.'

Leila jerked her gaze up. Alix's voice was quiet but his words had a profound effect on her. He sounded so... *protective.*

Before she could truly analyse how that made her feel she saw that they were driving into a car park outside a beleaguered-looking building.

Alix grimaced slightly as he pulled to a stop. 'The hospital doesn't look like much, but it houses some of the best consultants in the world. I've personally put many of our medical students through college for this very purpose— to bring them home to work and teach others. We're in the process of building a new hospital on a site nearby, and this one will be pulled down once it's built.'

Once again Leila was surprised to discover the depth of Alix's commitment to his island. And to discover how little she really knew him.

He got out of the Jeep along with a flurry of movement from the cars before and behind them, and as Alix solicitously helped her out she saw staff lining up to greet them.

Alix kept hold of her hand and Leila figured that of course he'd want to project a united front. Promote the fairy tale that they were in love.

She was introduced to the staff and the doctor who would be taking care of her prenatally—a genial older man. And then she was whisked away to be prepped for the scan, leaving Alix behind talking to the staff. The nurse was shy and sweet, and Leila did her best to put her at ease even though her own nerves were jumping.

What if they found something wrong?

When she was dressed in a gown and lying on a bed the doctor came in with Alix. He was chatty and warm, but Leila couldn't help her nerves mounting as cold gel was spread on her belly.

She glanced at Alix, but he was looking intently at the monitor where the doctor was focusing his attention as he moved the ultrasound device over Leila's belly.

She winced a little as he pressed in hard and almost reached for Alix's hand—some reflexive part of her was craving his solid strength and support. Instead she curled her hands into fists and looked at the monitor too. Her mother had done this alone. And even though Leila's baby's father was beside her she might as well have been alone too, for all the emotional support he was offering.

Suddenly a rapid beat filled the room, and it took Leila a second to figure out that it was the baby's heartbeat.

The doctor smiled. 'He—or she—is strong, that's for sure.'

A shape was appearing on the screen now, like a curled-over nut. The head was visible. And the spine. So delicate and fragile, yet there. Growing. Becoming someone. A son or a daughter.

Emotion suddenly erupted in Leila's chest and she had to put a hand to her mouth to stop a sob escaping. The love she felt, along with a fierce protectiveness, made her dizzy. Up to now it had been largely an intellectual thing. But this was visceral and all-consuming. *Primal.*

The doctor was saying reassuringly, 'Everything looks fine to me. We'll have you back in another few weeks, to see how things are progressing, but for now just eat well, take some gentle exercise and get lots of sleep.'

Leila just nodded at the doctor, too emotional to speak.

He patted her hand, as if he saw this every day—which he probably did.

When Leila felt a little more composed she looked at Alix. But even steeling herself didn't prepare her for seeing the closed-off expression on his face. His eyes were unreadable. He certainly wasn't feeling the same depth of emotion Leila was experiencing, and it was like a physical blow.

His gaze was still fixed on the screen, and then he seemed to come out of the trance he was in and he said curtly, 'So everything is fine, then?'

'Yes, yes…nothing to worry about.'

'Good.'

He didn't look at her. His jaw was hard, resolute. They'd established that the baby was well. That was all he cared about. Leila was far too emotional to deal with Alix's smug satisfaction now, and she welcomed the distraction of the nurse coming to help her change back into her clothes.

The doctor and Alix left, and Leila did her best to ignore the ache in her throat and the hollow hole in her chest. She'd never really imagined what this experience would be like, but even if she had she would have expected the father of her child to be slightly more interested.

This had obviously just been a clinical experience, as far as Alix was concerned. And she was a fool to have had even the minutest impulse to seek anything from him.

That protectiveness that had assailed her moments ago surged back at the thought of Alix being so distant once the baby was born.

Once she emerged into the corridor her ire increased when she saw Alix pacing up and down, on his phone. As if they'd *not* just established that their baby was well. He saw her and gestured to say that they were leaving.

She had to almost trot to keep up with his long-legged stride, and with each step she felt angrier and angrier and more *hurt*.

Alix terminated his phone call once they were in the Jeep and silence reigned. Leila was determined not to break it, feeling far too volatile and emotional. She knew Alix was sending her glances, but she resolutely ignored him, looking at the pretty scenery but not taking it in.

When they pulled up outside the castle she opened her door and got out before he could do it—or anyone else. She all but ran back into the huge stone fortress and blindly made her way down corridors, hoping she was headed in the right direction.

Everything was bubbling up—her hurt, her unwelcome desire for Alix and the need to get far away from the man who had turned her world upside down.

She heard steps behind her. 'Leila, what the—? *Stop!*'

She did stop then, breathless and hopelessly lost. She turned to face Alix, who was glowering. Fresh anger bubbled up, and again that fierce protectiveness. She felt the walls of the massive building crowd in on her, squeezing her chest tight. But biggest of all was the *hurt*.

She put a hand on her belly. 'You didn't feel a thing in that scan room, did you? Except maybe a sense of satisfaction that your precious heir is fine.'

Alix looked at Leila. She'd never been more beautiful. Her cheeks were flushed with colour, eyes sparkling with anger. And with something else that he didn't want to identify.

He saw movement in his peripheral vision and, aware of staff nearby, strode forward, taking Leila's arm in his hand. 'Not here.'

He looked around and saw a doorway, recognised what

it was. He opened it and brought a resisting Leila in, shutting the door behind him.

She ripped her arm free of his hand and moved away, looking around, her cheeks flushing even more and her eyes going wide as she took in the lavish surroundings.

'What is this place?'

Leila's voice was shaky and Alix hated the fact that it twisted his guts. He strode forward into the room. It was an opulent stone chamber with a raised marble platform. Alcoves around the edges of the room held sinks and drains. The ceiling was domed, and inlaid with thousands of mosaic mother-of-pearl stars that glittered.

'It was the women's *hammam*. And the harem is in this section of the palace too.'

Leila sent him an incredulous look. 'A harem? I thought we were still in the civilised west—not some medieval desert kingdom.'

Alix pushed down his irritation. 'The harem hasn't been in regular use for some time.'

Leila let out a laugh. 'Wow, *that's* reassuring. But maybe you're contemplating starting it up again? Taking additional wives just to fulfil your royal quota of children?'

Alix's jaw was so tight it ached, and yet he couldn't stop a series of images forming of Leila being stripped, massaged, washed and dressed by an army of women. And of him coming here to these secret and sensual rooms to find her waiting for him. Supplicant.

He wanted her so badly right then that he shook with it. He curled his hands into fists and said, 'Want to discuss what that was all about?' He couldn't even articulate himself properly. This woman tied him into knots.

She folded her arms over her breasts and it only served to remind Alix that he kept noticing how much fuller they were. The wrap dress she wore accentuated every womanly curve. He'd found it near impossible not to look at her bared belly in that room in the hospital, his control feeling far too flimsy.

'I'm talking about the fact that you might as well have been looking at a weather report in the hospital... Did seeing our baby on that screen affect you at *all*?'

CHAPTER TEN

ALIX LOOKED AT HER. *Did seeing our baby on that screen affect you at all?* His mind reeled. It had affected him so much he'd almost doubled over from the rush of pride, mixed with love and an awful bone-numbing sense of terror. Terror that something would happen to that fragile life that wasn't even born yet. Terror that something would happen to Leila. Terror at the surge of an emotion he'd never expected to feel again.

Leila didn't wait for him to speak. 'You were so cold... impervious. I will *not* bring a baby into a marriage where there is nothing between us except a sense of responsibility and duty. It's obvious you feel nothing for this baby beyond valuing it for the fact that it will inherit—'

Alix put up a hand, stopping her. Her words scored at his insides and yet he couldn't let it out—it was too much. And all he could see was *her*. So beautiful, so vital, and *here*. In front of him. Pushing his buttons.

Suddenly Alix wanted all the turmoil he felt to be consumed by fire. He moved closer to her and was gratified to see the pulse grow hectic at the base of her neck. Her breasts swelled with her breath.

'You say there's nothing between us?'

She nodded her head jerkily. Not so sure of herself now. 'There isn't. You only pursued me to distract people from your plans. You used me. You don't want me—you just want a vessel for your heirs. And it's not enough—for me or the baby.'

Alix was so close to Leila now he could smell her scent. Her unique brand of musk and sweetness.

'You're wrong, you know.'

Something flared in her eyes—something that once again he didn't want to identify.

'How?' she asked defiantly.

Alix reached out and took a lock of long, dark, glossy hair, winding it around his finger, tugging her gently towards him. She resisted.

'There *is* something between us and it's enough to bind us together for ever.'

He saw Leila swallow. He tugged her hair again and she jerked forward slightly, almost against her will.

'You see, I *do* want you. I wanted you the moment I saw you. I have ached with wanting you for the past seven weeks. And I am afraid that I will never stop wanting you, no matter how much I have of you—*damn you.*'

And with that Alix's control snapped and he hauled Leila into his arms, driving his mouth down onto hers, crushing her soft abundant curves to his body that was aching with need to be embedded in her tight, hot warmth.

Leila's brain fused with white-hot heat and lust. For long seconds she felt only intense relief as Alix's mouth crushed hers and he finally relaxed enough to allow the kiss to deepen and become a real kiss.

Then Leila's brain finally cleared enough to recall his words: *I have ached with wanting you.* Just like her. And now that ache was finally being assuaged.

Alix's big hands were roving over her back and waist, finding her hips, squeezing. Cupping her bottom, lifting her against him so that the hard ridge of his erection slid against her...just *there*.

She moaned into his mouth, rubbing herself against him, wanting more. She was incoherent with lust. Warning bells telling her to stop and think about what they'd just been saying to each other were being drowned out, and Leila knew that she was complicit in this.

She also knew that she was proving some point for Alix—and it wasn't necessarily a point she wanted to prove. But it was too late. She needed him too badly. She needed *this*. Physicality. No words or confusing emotions or hurt. Just the satisfaction of needs being met. Transcending everything.

Alix broke the kiss and drew back. He yanked aside the material of her dress to expose her breast, encased in lace.

Leila bit her lip to stop herself from begging. She was only still upright because one of Alix's arms was around her. Her legs were like jelly. And now he was pulling down the lace cup of her bra, freeing her breast and thumbing her nipple, then squeezing it gently.

She was so sensitive there that she almost screamed, circling her hips against Alix, utterly wanton.

He looked at her, his eyes flaming dark silver with need. A need that resonated within her too.

In a swift move he lifted her into his arms before she knew what was happening. Her shoes fell off as Alix strode out of the main *hammam* room and deeper into the harem. It was dark and shadowy. Mysterious. Rooms led off the corridor all in different colours.

He shouldered open one door and Leila's eyes went huge when she took in an enormous circular bed, dressed in blood-red silks and satins. The walls were covered with murals and it took a second for it to sink in that the murals depicted *Kama Sutra*–like explicit drawings.

A courtyard filled with wild blooming flowers was visible through French doors and a brightly coloured bird flew away from a water fountain. It was as if this was some kind of fairy tale and these rooms had been suspended in time all these years.

And then Alix laid Leila down on the bed and she knew this was no fairy tale. He was too intent…serious. Focused. And she knew she should care…should be getting up, walking away…but she couldn't move. And, worse, she didn't want to.

If this was all they had then she wanted it as fiercely as he did. Somehow, here, with Alix stripping off his outer urban layer, Leila could pretend that nothing else existed. For a moment.

When Alix was naked he lowered himself over Leila on his arms and dropped his head, his mouth feathering hot kisses along her jaw and neck down to where her pulse beat like a drum, sucking her there and biting gently. As if he wanted to leave his mark on her.

She reached for him, groaning with deep feminine satisfaction when she found his hard muscles, the defined ridges of his abdomen. And she reached down further, to where his erection jutted proudly from his body. Hot and hard. Silk over steel.

She wrapped a hand around him, suddenly more confident than she'd ever been before. She stroked him, loving how the muscles in his belly tightened at her touch.

Then he put a hand over hers and drew it away. 'I'll explode if you keep touching me like that. I need you—*now.*'

Suddenly Leila was frantic with the same urgency, and aware that she was still fully dressed—albeit with her dress gaping open and her bra pulled down.

Alix undid the tie of her dress and Leila wriggled out of

it. Her bra was dispensed with and Alix pulled her panties and tights down and off.

He stood back for a moment and just looked at her. Waves of heat made her blood throb and her skin feel tight. And then he came over her again, nudging her legs apart. He lavished attention on her breasts, sucking her nipples into his mouth and making them wet and tight with need. Then he trailed his mouth and tongue down over her belly, where their baby was nestled in her womb.

He seemed to linger there for a second, and Leila felt a rush of emotion, but she bit her lip to stop it coming out, afraid of what she'd say. And then she couldn't think, because Alix's mouth was moving lower, and so was he, hitching her legs over his shoulders and gripping her buttocks as he put his mouth on her *there*.

At the hot, wet seam of her body where she couldn't hide how much she wanted him.

She felt utterly exposed, but couldn't stop him as he stroked her with his tongue, opening her up to his ministrations, and then he found that cluster of cells and licked and sucked until she was gripping his hair and bucking towards his mouth, and his tongue was thrusting deep inside her.

And even though she'd climaxed, right into his mouth, it wasn't enough. She was panting, almost sobbing as he rose up like some kind of god. Her legs flopped wide and Alix moved his erection against her. After an enigmatic second of silent communication he thrust deep into her core. And her world shattered into pieces for a second time.

She became pure sensuality—engulfed in a never-ending moment of bliss. Alix moved within her, deeper and harder with each thrust. She was boneless, and yet she couldn't help the rising tide of another climax. Even after the last two.

She caught a glimpse of something above them and looked up. The ceiling was mirrored glass. Old and dark. But she could see Alix's sculpted and muscular buttocks moving in and out of her body, her legs wrapped around him, ankles crossed over the small of his back.

And it was as she saw his huge, powerful body flexing into hers with such beauty and strength that she fell apart for the third time, her orgasm so intense that she barely felt the rush of Alix's hot release, deep in her body, as he jerked spasmodically with the after-effects of his own climax.

When Leila woke she was completely disorientated. She was alone on the huge circular bed and the covers were pulled up over her chest. She could see herself reflected in the ceiling and her hair was spread around her head. Images came back… The sheer carnality of their union. The humiliating speed with which she'd capitulated.

'You're awake.'

Leila tensed and lifted her head. Alix stood by the open French doors of the room. It was dusk outside and birds called. The scent of the flowers was heady. Leila had to block out the immediate instinct she had to assimilate the smells.

She pushed herself up on her elbows, noting that Alix was in his trousers, but still bare-chested. 'Yes, I'm awake.'

She felt as if she'd been turned inside out. She tried to claw back her sense of anger from earlier, but it was hard when she felt as if someone had drained every bone from her body and injected her with some kind of pleasure serum.

She saw her dress at the end of the bed and sat up, holding the sheet to her as she reached for it. She put it on awkwardly, aware of Alix's intense regard, and tied it around her, sitting on the edge of the bed.

'You asked me earlier if it affected me, seeing the baby today?'

Leila went still and nodded.

'Of course it affected me. What kind of man would I be if I couldn't see my own child and feel something?'

Leila stood up, hoping her legs wouldn't fail her. She needed to move away from the bed—the scene of where she'd lost control so spectacularly. She saw a chair nearby and sank onto the edge.

'Why didn't you say something?'

Alix was terse, tense. 'Because I couldn't. It was too much all at once.'

Leila felt a very fragile flame of hope light within her. 'That's how I felt too. But when I looked at you, you were so closed off—as if you were just checking something off a list. I'm afraid that you won't love this baby. That it'll just be a means to an end for you.'

Like this marriage.

Alix looked as if he'd prefer to eat nails than pursue this conversation, but eventually he said, 'I should tell you about my brother.'

Leila frowned. 'You told me he was killed—with your parents.'

Alix nodded. 'Max was handicapped. A lack of oxygen to the brain when he was born prematurely. He wasn't severely disabled, just enough not to be able to keep up with kids his age. I was five when he was born. He spent a lot of time in hospital at first, in an incubator. My parents weren't interested, so I spent most of my time with him.'

Leila's heart lurched. She could imagine Alix as a serious, dark-haired five-year-old, with both his parents God knew where, keeping an eye on his brother.

'It was obvious to our father that he'd never become King, so he had nothing to do with him after that.'

Leila hid her shock. 'And your mother?'

His mouth twisted. 'She barely knew *I* existed, never mind Max.'

'He must have loved you very much.'

If anything Alix looked grimmer. 'He did, the little fool, following me everywhere… But I couldn't give him what he needed most: our parents' care and love.'

Leila sensed his reluctance to talk, even though he'd brought it up. But she needed to know this—because if they were to have a life together she couldn't bear for him to shut their children out.

'What happened the day he died?'

'They murdered him…' Alix moved a hand jerkily. 'Not just the actual murderers, but my parents. *They* were the ones who made sure I was protected so the precious line would go on, and *they* kept Max with them, knowing that he would die, hoping that seeing him would distract the soldiers enough to let me get away. The last thing I remember hearing was Max, screaming for me. He couldn't understand why I wasn't coming to get him, to take him with me—and I couldn't go back…they wouldn't let me. One of the men taking me away had to knock me out. I came to on a boat, leaving the island behind.'

He looked at Leila.

'It nearly killed me, knowing that I'd left him behind. I had nightmares for years. Sometimes they still come…'

Leila stood up. 'Oh, Alix… I'm so sorry.'

She could understand in an instant how something must have broken inside him that day when he'd lost his home and his beloved brother. She was going to walk over to him, but something in his expression stopped her.

Alix was harsh. 'Don't give me your pity, Leila, that's

the last thing I want or deserve. I've told you this because you need to know that I wasn't unaffected today. But I won't lie to you. I have always envisaged myself keeping an emotional distance from my Queen and any children. My role as King is a *job*, and as such I need to avoid distraction. Focus on what's best for the country and the future. But when I saw the scan today it all came back—the love I felt for Max and the awful grief when he died.'

Alix shook his head.

'It terrifies me that I'll be unable to control how I feel about my own child in case anything happens. I couldn't survive that grief again.'

A gaping hollow seemed to open up in Leila's chest. What could she say? Wasn't every parent terrified of their child being hurt or worse? Terrified that they wouldn't be able to protect it from every little thing? What Alix didn't understand yet, and what she only had an inkling of herself, was that he wouldn't be able to control it.

He walked over to her then, and Leila tried desperately to call up some sense of defence. She felt raw with this knowledge, not sure what it meant now.

'I want you, Leila, and I want our baby. I will do my best to serve you both well—and any other children we may have.'

Leila went still. Nothing had changed. Not really. Even though he'd opened up to her his main concern was the baby. Not her. And she should be feeling relieved that he'd admitted he wanted this baby as much for itself as for its role as heir. That he would not shut it out.

Alix reached a hand out then, but Leila stepped back jerkily. If he touched her now she'd break into a million pieces.

She forced herself to sound far more calm than she felt. 'I'm quite tired now. I'd like to go back to my rooms, please.'

Alix still felt raw from the mind-blowing sex and what he'd just revealed about his brother. But he hadn't been able to bear the thought that Leila really believed he'd felt nothing for their baby. And she deserved to know the truth. That he wasn't prepared to go through that emotional wasteland again. Having lost everything.

His hand was out to touch her, but she'd stepped back out of his reach. His first instinct was to move closer... but something stopped him. If he touched her again who knew what else he might feel compelled to reveal?

His hand dropped. He'd never wanted a woman so badly that he wanted her again as soon as he'd had her, but right now he really could see no end in sight to this constant craving.

The lush surroundings of the old harem didn't help. And the fact that *she'd* been the one to step away made something prickle inside him. She had control when he was in danger of losing it.

He was terse. 'Okay, let's go.'

Alix put on the rest of his clothes and watched Leila step into her panties, sliding them up her slim thighs. Thighs that had been wrapped around him only a short time before, her inner muscles clasping his shaft with spasms so strong he'd almost climaxed twice in quick succession.

Damn.

She picked up her shoes on the way out and Alix was forced to feel a measure of shame. They were like teenagers, sneaking off to the nearest private space to have sex. He was a *king*, for God's sake. Not a randy schoolboy.

'What are you going to do with this place?' Leila asked as she walked out through the main door.

He watched as she went past him, his eyes tracking down her body and up to her tangled hair. Lust was sinking its teeth into him all over again.

'I had thought of getting rid of it, but now I'm not so sure.'

She looked at him, and before she could say anything he stepped up to her, so that there were just centimetres between their bodies. 'It won't be for more wives, Leila, it'll be for us alone,' he said.

Her cheeks coloured at that. 'But that's…outrageous. A whole *hammam* and harem, just for two people?'

Alix quirked a smile at the mix of expressions on her face: slightly scandalised, and yet interested at the same time.

'It'll be purely for your pleasure and mine, Leila. You're to be my Queen, and I will want to make sure that you are satisfied.'

The colour faded from her cheeks and she said, 'I'll be satisfied when you don't shut our child out, Alix. Sex is just sex.'

Alix felt her words like a physical blow to his chest. He watched as she stepped out from where he had her all but caged against the wall and started to walk down the corridor. *Sex is just sex.*

'Leila,' he called out curtly.

She stopped and turned around with clear reluctance.

'It's this way.' He pointed in the opposite direction and watched as she came back down the corridor and past him, head held high. He had to stop himself from hauling her back into the harem to show her that he knew *exactly* that sex was just sex.

The irritating thing was he didn't *need* Leila to tell him sex was just sex. So why did he suddenly feel a need to prove that to her—and himself?

Leila wasn't sure how she made it back to her rooms with Alix behind her, boring holes in her back with the intensity of his gaze. She thought of that harem, existing just for carnal pleasure... She'd almost melted on the spot when he'd said that it would be solely for their use.

Sex is just sex—ha! Who was she kidding when she felt upside down and wrung out?

It had brought up all the emotions she'd been feeling the morning after they'd returned from Venice, when she'd felt so perilously close to believing she'd fallen for him.

There was no 'falling'.

The truth hit her like a slap in the face. She was in love with Alix and had been for some time, if she was honest with herself. And that last bout of *just sex* had left her nowhere to hide.

She almost sobbed with relief when she saw their door appear and the guard standing outside.

When they reached her room she was about to escape inside when Alix said, 'Wait.'

Leila turned around, schooling her features. No way would Alix know that what had just happened had been cataclysmic for her.

'Yes?' Reluctantly she looked at him, and saw his eyes were like grey clouds.

'We're having an engagement party at the end of this week. It's a chance to introduce you to society here, and there will be some international guests.'

Immediately nerves assailed Leila. She was a perfumer, a shop manager—not someone who walked confidently among the moneyed classes. Royalty!

But she needed space from Alix to process everything that had happened so she just nodded nonchalantly and said, 'Okay—fine.'

And then she slipped into her room and leant back against the door, letting out a long, shuddering breath.

She was in love with a man who had admitted to her that he was averse to love—based on the fact that he'd suffered so much pain due to losing his beloved brother. She could understand his trauma—and he would have felt it that much more keenly, being young and impressionable. But who was she to say to him that he wouldn't be able to control who or how he loved?

And yet he was willing to do his best for the sake of their child. Clearly that would have to be enough—and it should be. Everything Leila did now was for the sake of this baby. Her own personal needs and desires were not important.

Yes, they are, you'll wither and die in this environment with no love, whispered a rogue voice.

Leila pushed herself fiercely off the door and ignored the voice. As much as she longed for a different life from the one she'd had with her mother, she'd be an absolute fool to hope, even briefly, that some kind of fairy tale might be out there.

She stripped off her clothes and stepped into a hot shower and tried not to think of how it had felt to have Alix surging between her legs, touching her so deeply that it had made a mockery of the words she'd spouted at him.

Sex is never just sex, crowed the same rogue voice.

She shut it out and blinked back the prickle of weak tears.

* * *

On the evening of the engagement party Leila was a bag of nerves. It didn't help that she'd barely seen Alix since their last conversation. But she'd welcomed the space—especially in light of what had happened. She'd been having lurid erotic dreams of the harem all week.

Alix had sent her messages and notes, explaining that he was caught up with political meetings and getting everything prepared for the wedding.

And Leila had been kept busy with lessons about the history of the island, along with etiquette classes, instruction on how she would be expected to behave as Queen. And with wedding dress fittings.

The magnitude of how radically her life was changing was overwhelming.

The last thing she needed was to see Alix and have him guess just how brittle she was feeling.

Her personal maid, Amalie, was just finishing dressing her now, and Leila winced a little at the increased sensitivity of her breasts—which only made her think of how it had felt to have Alix's mouth on her there.

Amalie obviously misread Leila's discomfort. 'Are you too hot, *mademoiselle*? Shall I open the doors?'

Leila shook her head quickly. 'No, I'm fine—honestly.'

She forced a smile and looked at herself in the mirror, not really recognising the sleekly coiffed woman in front of her and feeling a moment of insecurity that Alix would take one look at her and feel nothing but disappointment with his inconvenient bride.

Alix stood in the doorway, unnoticed for the past few minutes, and watched as Leila was transformed from beautiful to stunning. His breath caught in his throat. She wore a cream strapless dress with a ruched bodice that clung to her full breasts before falling in delicate chiffon layers to the floor. Her dark hair was coiled into a complicated-looking chignon at the back of her head. Make-up subtly enhanced her eyes and that lush mouth.

Alix's body reacted with predictable force. A force he'd spent the week avoiding by keeping busy at all costs. Like some kind of yellow-bellied coward. He'd stood face to face this week with one of the men who had shot his parents and his brother, and he hadn't felt half the maelstrom he was feeling now.

As if sensing his regard, Leila turned her head and saw him. Her cheeks flushed and Alix gritted his jaw to stop his body reacting even more rampantly. He felt like a Neanderthal. He wanted to throw her over his shoulder and carry her back to the heart of that harem, to sink himself so deep he'd never have to feel or think again. He wanted to lock them in there for a month.

He stepped into the room with a velvet box in his hand, vaguely aware of the young maid curtseying and disappearing.

Leila looked from the box to him. 'More jewellery?'

She said it as if it was a poisoned chalice, and bleakly he had to realise that perhaps that was what this marriage was for her.

Alix curbed his irritation. 'Yes, more jewellery.'

He came closer to Leila and opened the box, watching her eyes widen at the sight of the exquisite gold necklace and matching earrings. He put it down and lifted the necklace, already knowing it would look stunning on her flawless olive skin. It was faintly geometric in design, and circular. He opened it and placed it around her neck, burningly aware of her body so close to his. Of his straining erection.

Leila put a hand to it as he took his own away and stepped back. 'It's beautiful. I don't mean to sound ungrateful. I'm just not used to...*this*. I feel like I'm not qualified.'

Alix saw her insecurity and was amazed at how little she was aware of her own beauty and power. *Over him*.

Gruffly he said, 'You're just as qualified as anyone else ever was. Most of the Queens in this family were slave girls, transported from northern Europe on ships, taken by pirates.'

Leila looked at him, a rare spark of humour in her eyes. 'That's one part of your history I *didn't* particularly relish learning about.'

Alix handed her the earrings and watched as she slid them into her ears. *Dieu*. He even found that erotic.

Feeling compelled, he said, 'I'm sorry I left you alone all week. I had things to attend to.'

It sounded so lame now. Pathetic. No woman had ever made him feel as if he wasn't in complete control. Except for this one.

He forced his mind back from the brink and stepped back. 'Ready?'

She nodded and he saw how she swallowed nervously. Instinctively he reached for her hand and led her out of the suite and into the corridor, aware of her tension and wanting to soothe it. Reassure her. Alien concepts for Alix.

They were coming close to where the sound of over two hundred guests could be heard and she stopped in her tracks. He looked at her and his chest squeezed at the fear on her face. *He'd* done this to her. He'd never contemplated having a wife who wouldn't just take this in her stride.

Her eyes were huge. 'What if I can't do this? I'm not a princess...'

Alix couldn't stop himself from reaching out and putting a hand to her neck, massaging her muscles with his fingers, feeling them resist and then relax. Her eyes were all he could see: huge pools of green. Her skin was so soft under his hand, and then he couldn't resist tugging her into him and lowering his mouth to hers.

They sank into each other, mouths open and tongues tangling, their kiss growing hotter and deeper before he had a chance to claw back some control. They were in the corridor. About to face guests. And he was ready to lift her against the nearest wall and thrust into her tight sheath.

Alix pulled back, feeling dizzy. Leila looked equally disorientated. Mouth pink and swollen.

Somehow he managed to grit out, 'You'll be fine. Just follow my lead.'

Leila wasn't sure how she was able to make her feet move at all after that kiss, but somehow Alix's words and his hand anchored her—although she had to figure that the kiss had been a somewhat calculated move to make her look suitably starry-eyed before they faced his public.

And then suddenly they were standing at the top of the stairs at the entrance to the majestic ballroom and Leila's nerves were back. It was filled with portraits of his rather fearsome-looking ancestors. The crowd started to hush as people noticed them. Alix took her hand and placed it on his arm.

A man in an elaborate Isle Saint Croix uniform struck a tall staff on the ground. It made an impressive booming noise and then he shouted out, 'May I present to you the King of Isle Saint Croix, Alixander Saul Almaric Saint Croix, and future Queen and mother of Isle Saint Croix, Leila Amal Lakshmi Verughese.'

Leila felt absurdly emotional at being called the mother of Isle Saint Croix as Alix led her down the stairs. She took a deep breath as they reached the bottom, and suddenly it was organised chaos as Andres appeared and led them around the room, introducing them to everyone.

CHAPTER ELEVEN

WHAT FELT LIKE aeons later, Leila wondered if her mouth would stay in a rictus smile for ever. Her cheeks ached and her feet were burning in the too-high heels. Thankfully the crowd had dissipated somewhat now, and she felt as if she could breathe again.

Alix's conversation with a man whose name Leila couldn't recall ended. He turned to her, looking genuinely concerned. 'Are you okay? You probably shouldn't be on your feet for so long.'

Leila had to stop her silly heart from lurching and forced a smile. 'Don't be silly—I'm pregnant, not crippled.' But in fact she *was* feeling a little hot and weary.

Alix was gesturing to a member of staff, giving him some kind of signal, and then he was leading Leila out to a secluded open courtyard off the main ballroom.

Leila sat down on a wrought-iron chair with relief, slipping off her shoes for a moment to stretch her feet. She caught Alix's look and said ruefully, 'Okay, my feet *were* beginning to kill me.'

The staff member appeared again, with a tray of hors d'oeuvres and some sparkling water. Alix sat down too and tugged at his bow tie, loosening it a bit.

More touched than she liked to admit, and surprised at

this show of concern, Leila said, 'You don't have to wait out here with me. I just need a moment.'

Alix popped an olive into his mouth and shook his head. 'I could do with a break myself. The French ambassador was beginning to bore me to death.'

Leila smiled and felt a moment of extreme poignancy, imagining that it could be like this—this sense of communion, sneaking out to take a break during functions. She quickly slammed the door on those thoughts. It was heading for dangerous fairy-tale territory again.

She helped herself to a vegetarian vol-au-vent and savoured the flaky pastry and delicate mushroom filling, more hungry than she'd like to admit.

'You need to eat more.'

She looked at Alix and grimaced. 'I'm still nauseous sometimes, but the doctor said it should ease off soon.'

Alix stood up then and looked out at the view. Something about his profile seemed so lonely to Leila in that moment—it was as if she might never truly reach him or know him. She found herself wondering if anyone ever had, and didn't like the sharp spiking of something hot and dark. *Jealousy.*

She forced her voice to sound light. 'Have you ever been in love, Alix? I mean with a lover.'

He tensed, and Leila found herself holding her breath.

'I've thought I was in love once before, but it wasn't love. It was only a very wounded youthful ego.'

Swallowing past the constriction in her throat, Leila asked, 'Who was she?'

Alix turned around to face her, leaning back against the wall. His expression was hard. 'I met her in America when I was a student. I thought she only knew me as Alix Cross. I was trying to stay under the radar and I believed that she was attracted to me for myself—not who I was...'

He leaned his hands on the stone wall.

'She was English. She'd come to America to escape the public scandal of her father gambling all their money away. They were related to royalty. She was looking for a way to get back into Europe and restore her reputation via someone else. Namely me. I was young and naive. Arrogant enough to believe her when she said she loved me. But the truth was that she just used me to get what she wanted. And clearly I wasn't enough for her, because I walked into her room one day and found one of my undercover bodyguards giving it to her a lot rougher than I ever could or wanted to.'

Leila looked at Alix's hard expression. *She just used me*. Her own words that she'd thrown at him came back to her like a slap on the face. *I used you*. She felt sick.

Then Alix said, 'I've already told you Max was the only person I've loved. I was brought up knowing any marriage would be a strategic alliance, all about heirs. I saw no love between my parents. Love was never part of the equation for me.'

That was what he'd said on the phone to Andres that day in Paris.

'I *can* promise to honour you and respect you, Leila. You did well this evening, and I have no doubt you'll make a great queen. And mother of our children. But that will have to be enough, because I can't offer any more.'

There it was—the brutal truth, sitting between them like a squat ugly troll. Dashing any hopes and dreams Leila might have had.

'Well,' she managed to say, as if her heart wasn't being lacerated in a million different places, 'at least we know where we stand.'

In a desperate bid to avoid Alix looking at her too closely, seeing the devastation inside her, she stood up too. She thought of what he'd said about being used and her conscience smarted. She really didn't want to do this, but his honesty compelled her to be honest too.

She went to the wall and mirrored his stance. 'I owe you an apology.'

'You do?'

Leila nodded and avoided his eye. 'That day in Paris… when I told you I'd used you just because I wanted to get rid of my virginity…I lied.'

She turned and looked at him, steeling herself not to crumble.

'The truth is that I *was* humiliated and hurt. I lashed out, not wanting you to see that.'

Something like a flash of horror crossed Alix's face.

Before he could say anything she cut in hurriedly, 'Don't worry. I wasn't falling for you… It was wounded pride. That's all.'

His expression cleared and Leila felt a monumental ache near her heart to see his visible relief.

'Look,' she said, putting a hand over her belly, 'all I want is to go forward from this moment with honesty and trust between us. At least if we have that we know where we stand, and it might be something we can build on. I won't deny that this marriage won't give me all that I need and want emotionally, but I'm doing this for our baby, and I'll try to make you a good queen.'

Alix looked at Leila and felt flattened by her words when only a moment ago he'd been feeling relief that she hadn't fallen for him.

This marriage won't give me all that I need.

And her admission rocked him. The fact that she hadn't meant those words, *I used you.* It ripped apart something he'd been clinging on to since he'd seen her again. As if as long as he had that he'd be protected.

She humbled him, this woman who had walked out of a shop and into a world far removed from anything she'd known, and she'd captivated the entire crowd this evening, behaving with an innate graciousness that he hadn't even known she possessed. She was putting everyone around her to shame.

Including him.

He felt like a fraud. He felt for the first time as if he was taking something beautiful and tarnishing it. He should let her go—but he couldn't. They were bound by their baby.

He owed her full honesty now.

'There's something you need to understand. When I met you I was consumed with nothing more than you. I never set out to use you as a smokescreen. There was no agenda. When we took that trip to Isle de la Paix it *was* spontaneous in that I planned it once you'd mentioned you didn't want any press intrusion. But I *did* see an opportunity, and I *did* arrange for someone to take that photo, seizing the chance to keep attention diverted.'

Alix sighed heavily.

'I had no right to exploit you for my own ends. And I'm sorry for that. Ultimately it led them straight to you. But when I pursued you it was because I wanted you— pure and simple.'

His admission made Leila feel vulnerable. If anything it just made things harder to know that he *hadn't* ruthlessly used her from the start.

She said, as breezily as she could, 'Well, it's in the past, and we're here now, so I think we just have to keep moving forward.'

Terrified he'd read something in her eyes, or on her face, she stepped around him and walked back into the ballroom.

She spent the rest of the evening avoiding him, in case

he saw how close to the surface her emotions were. Emotions that she'd denied she felt right to his face.

She knew they'd agreed to be honest, but there was such a thing as taking honesty too far. And Leila hated how this new accord made her feel as if they'd taken about ten steps forward and twenty back.

She realised that if she was to negotiate a life living with a man who could never—*would* never—love her, she was going to have to develop some hefty self-protection mechanisms.

'She's a natural, Alix. If you'd seen her... The kids loved her. The nurses and doctors are in awe of her. She's possibly done more for Isle Saint Croix in one visit to the children's ward of the hospital than you could have done in six months. No offence.'

Alix grimaced as he recalled his recent meeting with Andres. Of course he hadn't taken offence at the fact that apparently his fiancée was indeed bound to be as perfect a queen as he'd expected her to be. When he'd believed she was falling for him. The fact that she'd assured him she *hadn't* been was like a burr under his skin now.

In the past few days, since the engagement party, Leila had thrown herself into doing as much as she could to learn about her new role. Alix had gone to her rooms at night to find her sleeping, and as much as he'd wanted to slide between the sheets and slide between her legs, something had held him back.

The same thing that had held him back the night of the party, when he'd left Leila at her door. He'd wanted her so badly, but after everything they'd said he had been almost afraid that if he touched her something would spill out of him—something much deeper than a mere climax. Some truth he wasn't ready to acknowledge yet.

'Your Majesty? Your fiancée is here to see you.'

Conjured up out of his imagination to taunt him?

He turned around. 'Show her in, please.'

Leila walked in and Alix felt that all-too-familiar jolt of lust mixed with something else. Something much more complex.

She looked pale.

Alix frowned, immediately concerned. 'What is it?' He cursed softly as he came around and held a chair out for her. 'You've been doing too much. I told Andres that you're busy enough with wedding preparations—'

She put up a hand and didn't sit down. 'No, I'm fine. Honestly. I enjoyed the visit to the hospital.'

Alix smiled. 'You were a big hit.'

She blushed and ducked her head, and Alix felt a pang near his heart. Her ability to blush and show her emotions was one of the things that had made him fall for her...

Alix went utterly still as the words he'd just thought sank in—and dropped like heavy boulders into his gut.

Alix was so quiet that Leila looked at him. The smile was gone from his face and he was deathly pale. She put out a hand. 'Alix...are you all right? You look like you've seen a ghost.'

He recoiled from her hand and a look of utter horror came over his face. Leila flinched inwardly. But, if anything, this only confirmed for her the reason why she needed to talk to him. She had to do this to protect herself.

At least over the past few days she'd discovered a real sense that perhaps she *could* be a queen, that she could relatively happily devote her life to the people of Isle Saint Croix and her children.

But in order to survive she needed to create a very firm boundary where Alix was concerned.

The fact that he hadn't made any attempt to sleep with her in the past few nights had left her feeling frustrated and relieved in equal measure. She knew physical intimacy without love would eventually crack her in two—or that she'd end up blurting out how much she loved him, and she couldn't bear to see that horror-struck look on his face again.

Alix retreated around the desk—as if he needed to physically put something between them. Leila tried not to feel hurt.

She steeled herself. 'I wanted to talk to you about something. About us. And our marriage.'

Alix sat down, still looking a little shell-shocked. Leila sat down too, twisting her hands in her lap.

'Go ahead.' Alix sounded hoarse.

'I am committed to doing my best to be a queen that you can be proud of, and I will love our child—and children, if we have more. I do believe that we can have a harmonious union, and that's important to me for the sake of those children—I expect you will want more than one.'

Alix frowned. 'Leila—'

She spoke over him. 'But apart from with our children, and promoting a united front for social occasions or events, I would prefer if we could live as separately as possible. I don't want to share rooms with you. And I would prefer if any intimacies were to be only for the sake of procreating. I will understand if that's not enough for you, but I would just ask that you be discreet in your liaisons, should you feel the need.'

Alix's face was getting darker and darker. He stood up now and put his hands on the desk. Leila tried not to move back, or be intimidated.

'Let me get this straight. You want to maintain a separate existence in private and we'll only share the marital bed for the purposes of getting you pregnant? And if I'm feeling the urge in the meantime I'm to seek out a willing and discreet lover?'

Leila nodded, telling herself that it hadn't hurt so much or sounded so ridiculous when she'd thought it all through in her head. But this was the only way she felt she could survive this marriage, knowing he didn't love her.

At least if she could create a family then she would have some purpose in her life—love and affection.

But all at once she realised that that was the most selfish reason in the world for creating a family.

Alix's mouth was a thin line. 'My father paraded his many mistresses around the castle and did untold damage to this country. I vowed never to repeat his corrupt ways—so, no, I don't think I'll be taking you up on your helpful suggestion to maintain a discreet mistress.'

He came around the desk and towered over Leila. She stood up.

'And, no,' Alix continued, 'I don't believe I *do* agree that we should maintain separate existences. I believe that you will share my bed every night, and I expect intimacies to be many and varied. Are you *really* suggesting that I am going to be forcing myself on a reluctant wife?'

Leila had to stop a slightly hysterical laugh from emerging. Of course he wouldn't have to force himself on a reluctant wife. Even now she felt every cell in her body straining to get closer to him. But, standing so close to Alix now, she realised that she'd actually completely underestimated her ability to survive even if she could maintain some distance from Alix. And of course he wouldn't agree to her admittedly ridiculous terms. What had she been thinking?

A sense of panic made her gut roil. 'Then I don't think I can do this, Alix. I thought I could, for the sake of the baby…but I can't.'

She felt weak, pathetic, selfish.

'What are you saying, Leila?'

She forced out the words. 'I'm saying that I want more than you can offer me, Alix. I'm sorry… I thought I could do this, but I can't.'

Terrified she'd start crying, Leila turned and hurried out of the room.

Alix looked at the door that had just closed and reeled. He had to recognise the bitter irony of the fact that Leila had more or less just outlined the kind of marriage that he'd always believed he wanted.

Space between him and his wife. She would be his consort in public and mother to his children. She wouldn't infringe upon his life in any other more meaningful way.

He might have laughed if he hadn't still been consumed by the terrifying revelation that made his limbs feel as weak as jelly. The rush of love he'd felt while watching that scan had been for Leila as much as for the baby. He'd just been blocking that cataclysmic knowledge out.

She had just said she wanted more. And the even more ironic thing was that *he* wanted more too. He suddenly wanted the whole damn thing—and it was too late.

The gods weren't just mocking him…they were rolling around the floor, laughing hysterically.

Leila was aware of the bodyguards, standing at a discreet distance, and was doing her best to ignore them. Her chest ached with unexpressed emotion. She had taken a Jeep and driven away from the castle, needing some space and time to breathe. She should have expected that she wouldn't be able to move without triggering a national security alert.

And even the stunning view from this lookout point high on the island was incapable of soothing her.

The sound of another vehicle came from the narrow

road and Leila heaved a sigh of frustration. She turned around. Really, this was getting ridiculous.

But her breath stopped in her throat when she saw Alix getting out of the driver's seat. He looked grim and went over to the bodyguards. After a couple of seconds they all got back into their vehicles and left.

When they were gone he looked at her for a long moment, and then came over. He stood beside her and gestured with his head to the view.

'On a clear day, with good binoculars, you can see both the Spanish and African coasts from here.'

Leila looked away from him. 'It's beautiful.'

'There are hundreds of shipwrecks around the island. It's my plan to use them as an incentive to get people to come wreck-diving. Part of the tourism package we're putting together.'

Leila's heart ached. 'The island is magical, Alix. You won't have a problem getting people to come.'

He turned to face her and said quietly, 'And what about getting people to stay? I wonder what incentive I could offer for that…'

Your love, Leila thought bleakly.

But she had to come to terms with the futility of her position and she said, 'I'm sorry. I overreacted just now. Of course I won't be leaving. I can't. Our baby deserves two parents, and a stable foundation. It was just…hormones, or something.'

Alix didn't say anything for a moment, and then he held out a hand. 'Will you come with me? I want to show you something.'

Leila hesitated a moment, and then slipped her hand into his, hating how right it felt even as a gaping chasm opened up near her heart.

Alix brought her over to the Jeep and she got into the

passenger side. She watched him walk around the front, her gaze drawn irresistibly to his tall, powerful form.

He drove in silence for about ten minutes, and then drove off the main road down a dirt track. They weren't too far from the main town, and Leila could just make out the castle in the distance.

After about a mile Alix stopped and got out. Leila got out too and looked around, but could see nothing of immediate interest. Alix led her over to where a vast area looked as if it was in the process of being cleared and levelled, even though there were no workmen at the site today.

'What's this?'

Leila looked at Alix when he didn't say anything immediately. He was so handsome against the sunlight it almost hurt. She could see that he truly belonged here, in this environment. And that somehow she was going to have to belong here too. And weather the emotional pain.

'It will be your new factory.'

Leila blinked, distracted. 'My new...*factory*?'

Alix nodded. 'The area is being cleared and I've lined up architects to meet with you and discuss how you want it designed and built. There's also room for a walled garden, so you can cultivate and grow plants and flowers. We have a huge range on the island, including a rare form of sea lavender. There's room for a greenhouse too, if you need it. You'll know more than me what you need.'

Leila looked around, speechless. The area was massive. And in this environment she could grow almost anything. What Alix had just said was almost too much to take in. She turned around and saw the island falling away and the sea stretching out to infinity. She was simply stunned.

Alix said worriedly, 'You don't like the site? It's too small?'

Leila shook her head and blinked back tears, terrified that once the emotion started leaking out it wouldn't stop. 'No, no—it's lovely…amazing.'

When she felt more in control she looked at him.

Her voice was husky. 'I thought you said I'd have other priorities—the baby, my role as Queen?'

Alix looked serious. 'Leila, you inhale the world without even realising you're doing it—it's part of you. You're led by your nose. I want you to be happy here. And I hope that this will make you happy. I know you want more… you deserve so much more…'

A slightly rueful expression crossed his face.

'And I need you to make me more of that scent, because I destroyed the bottle you gave me in Paris. I destroyed it because I was angry and hurt.'

Leila's heart gave a little lurch. 'You weren't hurt. Your ego was wounded because I dared to say no to you.'

Alix nodded. 'That's what I believed. That it was my ego. Except it was a lie that I told myself and kept telling myself, even when I saw you again. The truth is that it wasn't just my ego—it was my heart. And I didn't have the guts to admit it to myself.'

He took her hands in his.

'It hit me today, Leila. Like a ton of bricks. I've been falling for you from the moment I saw you in your shop. When we were leaving Isle de la Paix I knew I had to let you go, but I didn't want to. I think I came up with the idea of proposing to you because it was the only way I could see to make you stay…'

Leila looked at Alix. She said a little dumbly, 'You're saying you *love* me?'

He nodded, looking wary now.

For a second Leila felt a dizzying sweep of pure joy—

and then a voice resounded in her head: *Silly Leila... there's no fairy tale.* The joy dissolved. She had thought the chasm in her chest couldn't get any bigger, but it just had.

She pulled her hands free. 'Why are you doing this? I've told you I'm not leaving.'

Alix frowned. 'Doing what? Telling you I love you? Because I do.'

Leila shook her head, those damn tears threatening again. 'I can't believe you'd be this cruel, Alix. Please don't insult my intelligence. I tell you that I want to go, that I don't think I can marry you, and now suddenly you're claiming to love me? You're forgetting I heard your conversation on the phone that day: *"If I have to convince her I love her then I will."*'

Alix ran his hands through his hair, his frustration palpable. Leila folded her arms.

'Why would I do this now? Pretend?'

Leila felt ill. 'You've made a very convincing case for persuading me that you're incapable of love, and now I'm suddenly supposed to believe you've had some kind of epiphany? It's three days to the wedding, Alix, and I know how important it is for you and for Isle Saint Croix, but I never thought you'd be unnecessarily cruel.'

Alix looked as if she'd just punched him in the gut, but Leila steeled herself.

He opened his mouth, but she said with a rush, 'Please don't, Alix. Look, I appreciate what you're trying to do—and all this...' She put out a hand to indicate the site for the factory. 'It's enough—it really is.'

It'll have to be. At least he didn't know that she loved him. It was her last paltry defence.

She turned away and started to walk back to the Jeep,

fiercely blinking back tears. She didn't see the way Alix's face leached of all colour as he watched her go. She also didn't see the look of grim determination that settled over his features.

Their journey back to the castle was made in tense silence. When they arrived Leila jumped out of the Jeep, but Alix moved faster than her and her hand was in his before she could react.

He led her into the castle, and when she tried to pull her hand free Alix only tightened his grip and looked at her, his face more stern and stark than she'd ever seen it.

'We have not finished this conversation, Leila.'

She had to trot to keep up with his punishing pace, and only recognised where they were when he opened a door.

Immediately Leila dug her heels in and pulled furiously on Alix's hand. 'I am not going in there.'

Alix looked at her and said tauntingly, 'Why, Leila? Sex is just sex, after all—isn't it?'

They were in the impressive *hammam* room before Leila could object and the door was closed. Alix stood in front of it, arms folded. She hadn't even registered him letting her hand go.

'You know, I never thought you were a coward, Leila.'

Leila's mouth opened, and she finally got out, *'Coward?* I am not a coward.'

Alix stepped away from the door and towards her. She eyed the door, wondering if she could make a run for it, and then his words sank in.

She couldn't run. So she rounded on him. 'What's that supposed to mean?'

He walked around her now, looking at her assessingly, and she had to keep turning, getting dizzy.

'You're a coward, Leila Verughese. An emotional coward. And I know because I was one too.'

Something like panic was fluttering in Leila's belly now. 'That's ridiculous. I'm not a coward and you're a liar.'

He arched a brow and made a low whistling sound. 'That's harsh. I told you I love you and you call me a liar?'

Leila changed tack. 'Why are you doing this? I've told you I'm happy to stay. You don't have to sweeten it up for me.'

Alix almost sneered now. 'You're "happy to stay"—like some kind of martyr? The days of pirates kidnapping European slaves and forcing them into marriage are over. When we marry it'll be because you want it as much as I do. Because you love me too—except you're too much of a coward to admit it. Why else would you want us to maintain a distance while we're married?'

Leila felt her blood draining south. Her last defence was crumbling in front of her eyes. 'I don't love you,' she lied.

'Liar.'

Alix stalked closer, tension crackling between them. 'If I'd been more honest with myself sooner I would have recognised it the day we left here—when you said sex is just sex. That was the key. Sex has *always* been just sex for me. Until you. That's why I haven't touched you since we were in here—because as soon as I touch you I'm not in control, and I was afraid you'd see it. And I think it's the same for you. *Dieu*, Leila,' he spat in disgust. 'You'd really want me to take a mistress?'

Leila could feel her insides tearing apart. 'But you don't love me—you can't. You said it.'

She sounded accusing now. The fairy tale was like a shimmering mirage, and she knew that the moment she committed herself to trusting, believing, it would disappear and she'd be left with less than she had even now.

Alix was ruthless. 'I can—and I do. You brought me to my knees and showed me that anything less than total surrender to love and all its risks is a life not worth living. It terrifies me, because I know how awful it is to lose someone you love, but I've realised that it's impossible to live in constant fear of that. I want more too—and I want it with you. No one else.'

Leila shook her head, tears making her vision blurry. It hit her then. Alix was right—she was a coward. Terrified to trust. Terrified that the dream didn't exist. Her mother's ghost whispered to her even now that it couldn't. She hadn't had it, so why should Leila?

Alix stepped right up to her. 'Say it, Leila.'

She shook her head. 'Please, don't make me…'

She had a terrifying vision of telling him she loved him only to see him go cold and shut down, satisfied that his convenient wife had surrendered to him completely.

Alix wrapped a hand around her neck. 'Then we do it this way… You're mine, body, heart and soul, and I will leave you nowhere to hide.'

Alix's head dipped and his mouth settled on hers like a scorching brand. Leila resisted. *This* was what she was afraid of, and suddenly speaking the words didn't seem so scary—what was far worse was the honesty he would wring from her now, because she literally would have nowhere to hide.

But it was too late for resistance. And Leila was weak. And again he was right. She *was* a coward.

She sobbed her anguish into his mouth as his tongue stroked hers and the flames licked higher and higher.

This time there was no way they could make it to the harem bedroom. Leila felt herself being lowered onto the raised platform of smooth marble. Their movements were not graceful or measured. There was a feral urgency to their coming together.

Clothes were ripped off. Alix's hands were rough, his mouth hard, teeth nipping and tongue thrusting deep into the slick folds of her sex. Leila's back arched. Her hands clenched in Alix's hair. His hands clasped her so tightly she knew she'd be bruised, but she revelled in it.

He was her man and she loved him.

And now he loomed over her, huge and awe-inspiring, face flushed and eyes glittering intensely. She saw the need on his face, making his features stark. She saw the uncertainty even now, in spite of his bravado, and her heart ached.

He sank into her body with slow and devastating deliberation, watching her. Demanding that she expose herself utterly.

Leila had nowhere to hide. He was true to his word. She wrapped her legs around him and finally broke free of the bonds of fear. He touched her so deeply she gasped and caught his face in her hands, the words spilling from her lips in a rush of emotion.

'Of course I love you, Alix. I love you with all my heart and soul. You're mine, and I'm yours, for ever.'

An expression of pure awe broke over his face. A look of fierce male satisfaction. And *love*.

Leila's heart soared free, and then the delicious dance of love started. And when Leila arched her back in the throes of orgasm and looked up, all she could see were thousands of glittering mosaic stars above their heads. And finally she believed in his love—deep down in the core of her body, where Alix had broken her apart and now put her back together.

EPILOGUE

LEILA HURRIED FROM the Jeep into the castle, greeting staff as she went in. Happiness and fulfilment were things that she felt every day now, but she didn't take them for granted for a second.

In the seventeen months since she'd married Alix, in a deeply emotional ceremony, they and the island had undergone seismic changes.

The island was thriving and growing stronger every day. Her factory had opened a few months ago and it, too, was beginning to flourish as she started to manufacture perfumes again. Her apartment in Paris was now an office over the shop, and she went back about once a month to keep an eye on proceedings.

She'd been stunned to get a call one day from her father's daughter—a half-sister. He'd been put under immense public pressure to do the DNA test which had proved his paternity of Leila and consequently ruined his political career. Leila's half-sister, Noelle, had confided that her and her brother's life had been blighted by his numerous affairs and their mother's unhappiness.

She'd already come to Isle Saint Croix to meet Leila, with a protective Alix by her side, and their relationship was tentatively flowering into something very meaningful.

But the real heart and centre of her life was right here in the castle. Everything else was a bonus.

When Leila walked into Alix's office she couldn't help a grin spreading across her face at the scene before her, featuring her two favourite people in the world. Alix and their dark-haired eleven-month-old son, Max.

Max was bouncing energetically on Alix's knee, simultaneously slapping his pudgy fists on the table while trying to cram what looked like a very mushed up banana into his mouth.

Alix had a big hand firmly around his son and was typing with one hand on his open laptop, safely out of destruction's way.

Then they both caught sight of her at the same time— two pairs of grey eyes, one wide and guileless, the other far more adult and full of a very male appreciation and love.

'Mama!'

Small arms lifted towards her and Leila plucked Max off Alix's knee. But before she could move away Alix's arm snaked around her waist and pulled her onto his lap. Max was delighted—clapping his hands, bits of banana flying everywhere.

Leila chuckled. 'I was trying to help you.'

Alix slid Leila's hair over her shoulder and pressed a kiss to her exposed neck.

She shivered deliciously and asked a little breathlessly, 'Where's Mimi?'

'I gave her the afternoon off. We were lonely without you—weren't we, little man?'

Max gurgled his agreement. Leila stood up and found a wet wipe to clean her son as much as possible, before putting him into his playpen and watching him pounce on his favourite cuddly toy.

She turned to face Alix, eyes sparkling, voice dry, 'I was in the factory for three hours and you got *lonely*?'

Alix stood up and took Leila's hand and drew her over to a nearby couch, pulling her down with him so she ended up sprawled on his lap again—this time in much closer proximity to a strategic part of his anatomy.

'I get lonely the minute you leave my sight,' he growled softly.

Leila's heart swelled. 'Me too.'

The playpen was suspiciously quiet, and Leila checked quickly to see their son sprawled on his back, thumb in his mouth, cuddly toy clamped to his side, fast asleep. Worn out.

She leaned back against her husband. 'I have something for you.'

He arched a brow and moved subtly, showing her that he had something for her too. 'Do you, now?'

She nodded and took a bottle from the pocket at the front of her shirt dress. The label read *Alix's Dream*. It was the perfume she'd first made for him. And one that was so personal she never sold it to anyone else.

He kissed her, long and slow and deep. 'Thank you.'

'Mmm,' she said appreciatively. 'I'll have to make it more often if that's the sort of response I'll get.'

Alix shifted so that she slid into the cradle of his lap. Leila groaned—half in frustration, half in helpless response. 'Alix…'

'I'm going to make a secret passage from here to the harem,' he grumbled.

Leila blushed to think of their very private space, which had been completely refurbished. The *hammam* was in use again too, and was open to local women and the women of the castle.

Leila loved going there amongst them and hearing their

stories. It was one of the things that had earned them both the love and respect of their people—their unaffected ways and their wish to be considered as equal as possible.

Alix teased a strand of Leila's hair around his finger. 'Andres said you went to the hospital today? Another visit to the new children's wing?'

Leila nodded—and then the excitement bubbling inside her couldn't be contained any more. 'Yes, but I also had an appointment to see Dr Fontainebleau.'

Alix immediately tensed at the mention of the royal doctor. 'Is there something wrong?'

Leila shook her head and took his hand, placing it over her belly. 'No, everything is very okay…but we'll be a little bit busier in about eight months.'

The colour receded from Alix's face and then rushed back. His arms tightened around her and then he lowered her down onto the sofa. His formidable body came over her, his happiness and joy palpable.

When he spoke his voice sounded a little choked. 'You do know that you've made me the happiest man in the world, and that I love you to infinity and beyond?'

Leila blinked back emotional tears and wound her arms around her husband's neck, drawing him down to her.

'I know, because I feel exactly the same way. Now, about that secret passage to the harem…do you think we could get it done before the baby arrives?'

* * * * *

Amanda Cinelli

Christmas at the Castello

'THERE'S STILL SOMETHING MISSING.'

Dara stood poised at the top of the staircase, looking over the Winter Wonderland theme that had transformed the opulent grand ballroom below her. Her assistant, Mia, waited patiently by her side. The younger woman had long ago got used to her boss's obsessive eye for detail. Devlin Events was about creating perfect Sicilian weddings for their high-profile clients. Over the past three years Dara had gained an army of the industry's most talented people and put them onto her payroll, but she still liked to oversee the final run-throughs at their most prominent venues. There was no one in the industry who could spot the little things better than she. And right now something was off.

Sweeping yet another glance around the room, she mentally checked off twenty-five tables, each adorned with a glittering crystal tree centrepiece. The overall effect was like a winter forest, with white and blue lighting completing the wintry theme. Her bride, a famous opera singer, had expressly forbidden any real flower arrangements on the tables. She had instead ordered hundreds of spherical arrangements of fresh white and pink roses, to be suspended from the ceiling in intricately symmetrical clusters.

Dara counted across the floating flower bombs—as she had so lovingly named them. She got as far as the third row before she noticed the problem.

She sighed. 'They've doubled up on the colours.'

Mia's head snapped up. 'Are you sure?'

'Right over here.'

She walked down the marble staircase, the click of her heels echoing on the hard surface. She came to a stop underneath the offending decoration. It wasn't a major issue, but it was damned irritating now she'd noticed it. Mia's quiet voice came from behind her.

'Should I fetch one of the guys from the ceremony room?'

Dara shook her head. 'The wedding is due to start in two hours—the ceremony room is priority.' She smoothed down the front of her sleek red pencil skirt, trying to focus on everything *but* the mismatched flowers above her. Her eyes drifted upwards again.

Mia laughed. 'I'll go and get somebody.'

She disappeared out through the door, leaving Dara alone in the glittering winter ballroom.

The rest of the room was perfect. Her team was talented, and very capable of doing most of the work unchaperoned. She could pick and choose which events to attend, leaving her plenty of time to travel with her jet-setting husband. But it had been three weeks since she and Leo had been together—his newest business expansion into Asia had kept him away much longer than usual.

The restlessness that had plagued her over the past months seemed to have intensified in the absence of her husband. Three weeks was the longest they had spent apart. She was unable to shake the feeling that something was wrong—or perhaps something was about to *go* wrong.

Their joint venture into charity work in Sicily kept her busy. The Valente Foundation was doing fantastic work in some of the most disadvantaged areas on the island.

And with Christmas fast approaching there was lots of volunteer work to do. But, as busy as she kept herself, something still kept her wide awake at night and staring at the ceiling.

Making a snap decision, she grabbed a ladder from nearby and set it up, removing her heels in the process. She didn't need to stand here waiting for a big strong man to fix the problem. There was no reason why she couldn't do it herself.

She quickly reached the top, keeping both hands in front of her on the cold metal for balance. It was true: if you wanted a job done well, sometimes you had to do it yourself. She focused on the arrangement, unhooking it from its place and lowering it down. It was heavier than she had expected, and she gasped as the world unexpectedly tilted on its axis.

'*Dio*, what *is* it with you and ladders?' a deep voice shouted from below her as the ladder suddenly righted itself and she was entirely vertical again.

'Leo.' Her heart gave a sharp thump.

Her husband was looking up at her, his hands holding the metal ladder steady. Dara dropped the flower arrangement and cursed.

'It's nice to see you still haven't lost your love of daring stunts, *carina*.'

Dara descended the ladder as quickly as she could manage and practically fell into her husband's arms. The familiar smell of him surrounded her, making her sigh involuntarily.

'Surprise…' he whispered huskily against her neck.

His permanent five o'clock shadow brushed against her skin and she shivered. Oh, how she had missed those shivers.

'You're a week early.' She pulled back in his arms.

He smirked. 'I like to be unpredictable.'

She loved it when he smiled like that, filled with mischief. Life was too serious without Leo around.

'I've got a surprise planned. Do you think you can manage a few days away from your work?'

'Right *now*? Leo, that sounds wonderful, but I'm needed here.'

Dara made a noise of protest, only to have him silence her with a finger against her lips.

'Do you remember your wedding vows, Signora Valente?'

Dara remembered their wedding day as if it had been yesterday. She had originally planned a simple ceremony on the beach in the Caribbean. But then they'd both realised there was only one place they could imagine becoming man and wife, attended by a few select family and friends: the *castello*, which had become the setting for the most romantic day of her life.

'We both agreed to remove that medieval part about obeying one's husband from our vows.' She raised a brow.

'I'm talking about the part where we promised to spend each and every day loving each other.' His gaze darkened as his hand drifted lower on her back. 'And it seems I've got about twenty-two days of loving to make up for.'

His mouth lowered to hers and captured it in a scorching kiss full of dark, sensual promise.

A muted cough interrupted them from their interlude. Mia, accompanied by one of the movers, stood awkwardly at the top of the stairs. Dara stood back from their sensual embrace, her cheeks flaming.

'Nice to see you home safe, Mr Valente,' Mia said and blushed. 'Shall I book you both into the restaurant for lunch?'

'I've come to steal my wife away, I'm afraid.'

Dara placed a hand against her chest, straightening her blazer as casually as she could manage under the scrutiny of her staff. 'Leo, I can't just leave two hours before an event—'

'Actually, you can,' Mia interrupted, blushing even more as both Leo and Dara turned to face her. 'What I mean is, Dara, you've been working so hard… What's the point in being the boss if you can't take some time off? The rest of the team can see this through perfectly well.'

Leo moved forward, grabbing Dara's shoes from the floor. 'Mia, you are the voice of reason.'

Dara shook her head, smiling. 'This is crazy. I have a million things I should be doing.'

'That's what makes stealing you away so much fun.' He winked, pulling her by the hand. 'Mia, you are only to call my wife if there is a fire or some other catastrophic event.'

'Understood, sir.' The assistant saluted, giggling uncontrollably as Leo commandeered his speechless wife from the room in her bare feet.

'Is the blindfold really necessary?' Dara asked, feeling for Leo's hand in the close confines of his sleek sports car.

'Necessary? Perhaps not,' Leo's voice purred silkily somewhere next to her ear. 'But it adds to my enjoyment.'

Dara reached out, her hand coming into contact with his arm: a band of hard muscle covered in the rich silk of his dark shirt. 'Well, in two years of marriage you've never mentioned this particular fantasy.'

Dara's breath whooshed out of her lungs as a warm hand settled possessively upon her inner thigh. It had been weeks since she'd felt her husband's hands on her body, and the sensation was just as addictive as she remembered.

'I've never been one for power plays, but I must say I am enjoying the effect so far,' he murmured seductively.

'I'm open to the blindfold, but I'm drawing the line at handcuffs,' she replied, focusing on the agonising slowness of his fingers as they progressed towards the hem of her skirt.

'We're hot enough in the bedroom without adding props, *carina*,' he rasped, gripping her thigh and squeezing gently. 'And I'm liable to stop this car on the side of the road if you don't stop making those delicious little noises.'

Dara smiled to herself, hearing his laboured breathing. 'I'll behave myself if it means avoiding an accident. Still, I'm not opposed to you being so out of control.'

He chuckled. 'I'll make note of that.'

Less than fifteen minutes later the car had moved off the motorway and onto rougher terrain. She had expected him to take her to the private airfield where they normally housed the jet, but he wouldn't have needed to blindfold her for that. The past Christmases of their relationship had been spent travelling abroad. Sipping champagne at the top of the Eiffel Tower...exploring deserted beaches in Bali. She wondered what on earth he had planned this year. Curiosity made her stomach jolt with excitement as she felt the car suddenly pull to a smooth stop.

Leo jumped out from the car, ordering her to wait as he opened her door and helped her out into the crisp night air. He gently removed the blindfold, allowing Dara a moment as her eyes adjusted to her surroundings.

She looked up at the familiar facade of Castello Bellamo and felt her breath catch. Thousands of tiny twinkling fairy lights adorned the steps to the double doors. The entrance glowed as though lit up by some kind of magical force.

'The real surprise is inside.' Leo took her by the hand and led her up the steps and through the open doors into the grand hallway.

The *castello* had always been a magical place to her, with its vaulted ceilings and mysterious corridors. But now it simply took her breath away. Thick garlands of flowers adorned each side of the staircase, and tiny ornamental elves sat on a side table surrounded by candlelight. The light from the chandelier above had been left dimmed for maximum effect, and she could see a warm glow emanating from the doorway leading into the front sitting room.

'Leo, the place looks like something from a fairy tale.' She sighed, wandering through the archway. Her breath caught as she took in the enormous Christmas tree that dominated the room. The tree had to be at least nine feet tall, and was perfectly decorated in an array of red and gold. 'Did you do this all by yourself?' she asked, still stunned by all the effort he'd gone to.

'I had some help,' he admitted. 'I remembered you spoke about how much you loved the traditional family Christmases you had as a child.' Moving his weight onto one foot, he leaned against the archway and watched her. 'Do you like it?'

Dara turned to him, feeling tears well up in her eyes as she realised that her powerful jet-setting husband was actually nervous.

'Leo, this is so thoughtful, I'm actually—' She swallowed down her emotion, trying not to ruin the moment with silly tears.

'What's wrong? Have I upset you?' Leo was by her side in an instant and enveloping her into his strong embrace. 'I know that we usually spend this time of year somewhere warmer and more exotic. Are you disappointed?'

Dara shook her head quickly, looking up into the brilliant emerald depths of his eyes. He was so serious, so concerned, and yet she couldn't seem to find the words to assure him that this was wonderful.

'It's perfect,' she rasped. 'Thank you.'

She felt his arms relax around her, pulling her closer into the wall of his chest. She tilted her head up and claimed his mouth in a kiss full of heat and promise.

Leo groaned and smoothed his hands down Dara's back slowly, allowing his hands to rest on her supple curves. She was still as addictive as ever, his wife. And he'd be damned, but he couldn't wait another moment before having her.

The soft rug before the fire made for an excellent makeshift bed. He lowered them both to the floor slowly, unbuttoning his shirt in the process. Dara began to pull at the buttons on her own blouse, but Leo had other plans. He laid a hand gently on top of hers.

'I've been fantasizing for weeks about undressing you,' he whispered sensuously as he ran a slow, torturous hand down her ribcage.

Dara shivered, heat rising in her cheeks. 'You still fantasize about me?' She looked doubtful.

'*Amore mio*, you are the only woman who gets me like this. Look at me—I'm rock-hard and struggling for breath after one kiss.'

Dara's eyes sparked with possession as she laid her hand on his belt buckle. 'I'm glad. Because I plan on being the only woman for a long time yet.'

Leo sucked in a breath as her fingers undid the buckle, lowering the zip of his trousers in one smooth movement. Her hand wandered, momentarily grazing his erection and making him groan.

'Such a tease,' he growled, pushing her back down onto the rug. 'This is *my* fantasy, remember?'

Leo grabbed the waistline of her pencil skirt, tugging it low on her hips before removing it completely. What he saw beneath made his eyes widen and his heart thump uncomfortably. Delicate thigh-high stockings covered her legs, held in place by a black lace garter belt.

'This is new.' He felt his throat run dry.

Dara's blush deepened. 'I had a feeling you'd like it.'

Leo ran his hand across the flimsy lace, feeling the heat of her skin underneath. A matching thong was the only thing that lay between his fingers and the moist heat of her delicate skin beneath.

'I planned to take my time...' He bit his lower lip, watching her eyes darken as she arched her hips against his hand. He leaned down, taking the lace between his teeth as he undid one catch and rolled the stocking slowly down the smooth skin of her thigh. Discarding it on the floor, he turned his attention to the other thigh and repeated the action. Dara shivered, unconsciously spreading her thighs wide for him. Or maybe it wasn't unconscious at all; maybe she was deliberately trying to drive him insane.

Pushing the thin lace to one side, Leo trailed one fingertip along the slick crease between her thighs. Dara moaned under his touch, pressing closer into his hand. He could tell that she was ready for him. But a wicked part of him made her wait a moment longer. He leaned just close enough to blow a single breath of hot air against her sensitive flesh.

Dara gasped, gripping the hair at the nape of his neck to pull him closer.

The action drove him wild. She was flushed and breathing harshly. Leo obeyed her breathless plea, pressing his lips to her tender flesh and hearing her groan in response. He moved his mouth in sync with his fingers, driving her closer and closer to that point of no return. He felt her body tense under the onslaught of pleasure. A single curse escaped those delicate lips as she reached her climax.

No sooner had her aftershocks subsided than he was thrusting deep inside her, sinking into her molten heat with a muttered curse of his own. 'Oh, *Dio*, I've missed this.' He groaned as he built up a steady rhythm, spreading her legs wide as he leaned down and took one taut nipple into his mouth.

Dara caressed his back with her fingertips as he drove into her with all the control he could muster.

His release came hard and fast, taking them both by surprise.

Once the wave of pleasure had subsided, he sank down on the rug by her side and exhaled hard.

Dara sat up on one elbow, tracing the hairs on his chest idly. 'That was worth the wait.'

Leo murmured his agreement, feeling her hands on his chest and listening to her rhythmic breathing as his eyes closed.

Dara couldn't sleep. She stared up at the two stockings that hung over the fireplace. They looked so plain, so small on that huge mantelpiece. That same feeling that had plagued her for the past few months threatened to overcome her again.

This wasn't about the stockings.

The same way as her frequent trips to Syracuse had nothing at all to do with business.

Since they had opened up their charitable project, the Valente Foundation, she had been required to attend a handful of fundraisers and benefits. Her presence wasn't necessarily required in any of the institutions they supported on a day-to-day basis, and yet she had found herself taking on the role of patroness at the Syracuse orphanage with the aim of being a silent figure.

The first couple of trips had been to check on the progress of some renovations, and then she had arranged for a new playground to be built. That playground had been finished in the summer, and yet she still found reason to visit as often as she could manage. With Leo away she had found herself making the hour-long trip up to three times · a week. Even the ever-smiling house matron had begun to look confused at her continued presence.

There were stockings up on the fireplace at the orphanage too. Seventeen of them, side by side, hanging on a string in the common room. Now that Leo was home she supposed she would find no reason to go to Syracuse again. He would ask questions about why she visited only one orphanage—why not all the others? Why not the hospitals? He would know, just as she knew, that her actions weren't about being charitable at all.

The press had been merciless in the beginning: everyone had wanted to see Leo Valente transformed from playboy to father. Dara had never made a secret of her inability to bear children, so it had been no surprise that the press had caught wind of it soon after their wedding. The rumour mill had gone into overdrive. Would they adopt? Would they use a surrogate? They'd been a hot topic for quite some time.

They had decided that their business was their own, and that their choice to remain childless was both private and definite.

Hot tears threatened to fall from her eyes now, as emotion built in her throat. It just didn't make sense. She had made it clear from the start—before they married—that children were not in her future. She'd made her peace with that on a hospital bed, upon being informed that her condition was incurable. She hadn't been foolish enough to hold out any hope of some day carrying a child of her own. It was better to be realistic. She had never had strong maternal tendencies anyway. For goodness' sake, she was a workaholic and a complete neat freak—both qualities didn't exactly mix well with motherhood.

She knew all this and yet she had been selfish enough to go back to the orphanage after that first time. Selfish and inconsiderate.

She had been plagued by a sense of restlessness these past few months. Married life was wonderful, and her success in her career was at an all-time high. And yet it seemed as if the only time she felt whole these days was when she was there.

The children were wonderfully well behaved, thanks to the efforts of the brilliant schoolteachers led by Matron Anna. Each visit brought with it new adventures filled with laughter. Life was less serious, less stressful.

A vision of small brown eyes and a playful grin filled her mind. A small hand holding on to hers so tightly. She couldn't keep lying to herself. There was only one reason why she kept going back there, and that reason had a mischievous smile and liked to curl up on her lap to read.

She heard the sounds of Leo waking up behind her and tried to wipe away the tears from her cheeks without him noticing. Tried and failed.

'Dara?' He was up in an instant, sleep clouding his eyes. 'Has something happened?'

'I'm fine—let's just go up to bed.' She shook off his embrace, pulling a blanket from the sofa to drape around her shoulders.

'You've been crying.'

'I'm fine…honestly.' She tried to avoid his penetrating gaze, turning to poke at the dwindling embers in the grate.

'You've been acting strangely since we got here. I thought you loved this place—I thought being here on a more permanent basis would make you happy.'

'It does. I'm looking forward to us spending Christmas here together.'

'Dara, I don't know what is going on with you. You've been avoiding some of my phone calls while I was away. Even when I specifically called when I knew you'd be finished with work. And today my driver mentioned that you've been disappearing by yourself for hours at a time. With no reasonable explanation—'

'You had your driver keeping tabs on me?' Dara was incredulous.

'I wasn't going to pay it any attention, because I trust you. But dammit, Dara, you're hiding something from me and I want to know what it is. *Now.*'

'What do you think? That I'm cheating on you?'

Leo crossed his arms, looking darkly into the glowing fire. 'I'd like to think I know you better than that.'

Dara placed her hands on her hips. 'Well, it sounds like you're accusing me of something. I'm entitled to *some* level of privacy. Just because we're married, it doesn't mean we need to live in each other's pockets, for goodness' sake.'

She moved to walk away and felt his hand move gently to her wrist.

'Dara…'

His voice was quiet, and something in its tone appealed to her logic. She knew she was behaving out of character. And that he must be concerned. He had flown for almost twenty-four hours to come here and surprise her, and here she was shouting at him for asking if she was okay.

The realisation brought even more tears.

'I'm sorry.'

She sat down heavily on the sofa, hiding her face in her hands. She felt him come to her, felt his solid warmth slide alongside her and envelop her as she sat there trying to make sense of why she was falling apart.

'I've been going to the orphanage in Syracuse,' she admitted. 'It started as a simple project to update their facilities. But then it became…more.'

Leo sat silently, watching her reveal her secrets.

'I was there one day, helping to choose wallpaper for the common room, when one of the smallest children—a boy—walked right up to me and grabbed my hand. The other children had avoided me on previous visits; I was a stranger with a foreign accent and a fancy suit. I was unapproachable.' She smiled to herself. 'But not him. He grabbed on to my hand and asked me to come and see his drawings. He had drawn a picture of a house by the sea. He gave it to me as a gift and asked me if I would come back again. So I did.'

Leo remained silent for a moment, watching her. 'Why do you feel the need to hide all this? It's charitable work.'

'Don't you see? It's *not* work to me. I *want* to be there. It makes me happy to be there with all the children. But most of all with Luca…'

'Luca is the boy's name?' Leo asked quietly.

Dara nodded. 'It's unfair of me to grow attached. Because he's just a child and he will think that I want to… that we might want to…' The words stuck in her throat, unable to come out.

'That you might want to become his mother?' Leo said.

Dara looked at him quickly, as though he had struck her. That one word was enough to make her mind turn to panic.

Mother.

'I won't go back again. I suppose I'm only just realizing that I've used the orphanage to relieve my restlessness. To occupy myself.'

She stood up and walked to the Christmas tree, touching one of the golden baubles and making it spin.

'It was a selfish act and I'm feeling guilty, that's all.'

Dara turned back to her husband. He sat completely nude on the sofa, watching her with a look so concerned it melted her heart. If she told him any more she would only regret it in the morning. It wasn't that she feared his judgement. In fact it was completely the opposite. She feared his pity.

Leo had taken the news of her infertility in his stride from the moment she'd revealed her secret to him. He had been understanding, and he had helped her to realize that her condition did not define her.

To bring up all those old insecurities now would only belittle how far they had come as a couple.

That was the thing, though—she wasn't quite so confident that she had ever rid herself of them at all. Rather, she had just chosen to focus on being the beautiful woman that Leo made her feel she was and ignored the sad and broken woman of her past.

She bit her lip. Leo was looking at her intensely, waiting for her to speak. She couldn't tell him the truth, not tonight anyway.

'I'm sorry. I feel like I've ruined this wonderful night with my own silly ramblings.' She shook her head, banishing the dark thoughts from her mind.

She walked to him and straddled his lap.

'Dara, we're having quite a serious conversation here, and I will find it very difficult to concentrate with you in this position.'

He shifted, but she moulded her body even closer to him.

'I've had enough talking for tonight.' She leaned over him, nipping his earlobe just hard enough to make him groan. 'You said we have twenty-two days to make up for, and I plan on obeying my husband's wishes.'

She smiled wickedly, banishing all other thoughts from their minds as their bodies instinctively moved against each other.

Leo sat on the terrace, looking out at the midday winter sun shining on the choppy waves of the bay. Most of their morning had been spent in bed, making up for lost time. But some time after brunch Dara had found herself taking a call from Mia about something vitally important. Rather than being annoyed at the interruption, Leo had once again been impressed at how much his wife's company relied on her.

She ran Devlin Events like a well-oiled machine—just as he would expect. But still her staff looked to her for guidance, and felt comfortable in doing so. This was one of the main reasons for her skyrocketing success. Her employees were satisfied, and therefore so were her clients. Add that to the fact that she was unbelievably talented and passionate, and it could only be a recipe for success.

He watched her through the terrace doors as she booted up her tablet computer and wielded it like a clipboard. She was tense, even after a night of being thoroughly made love to.

Her revelation about her trips to the orphanage had confused him. Dara had never shown any interest in children. He had never even seen her speak to a child, not to mention drive out of her way to go and visit one. But recently he had begun to feel a distance between them.

They both had busy careers, but they usually made sure to keep time for each other.

Leo stood, suddenly needing to walk. He took the path down along the cliff-face—the same path he'd used to take as a boy. He stopped on the flight of steps that led down to the old boathouse, remembering his childhood self rushing down the stone steps, furiously trying to hold in the tears and escape his nightmarish life. Living with a mentally ill mother had forced him to live in silence. His formative years had been spent in isolation, and in fear of upsetting her with his mere presence.

Those memories no longer held the same dark power over him—not since Dara had come into his life. Now every time he walked down here he was reminded that he was happier than either of his parents had ever been.

Right now, he was impressed that the little boathouse was still standing. He pushed the door open with a creak and ducked his head inside.

A row of plastic boxes lined the floor—he had insulated the place last year, once they had decided to use it for storage rather than leave it to rot. Flipping the lid of the box nearest the window, Leo idly surveyed the contents. A collection of coloured yo-yos lay inside, once his favourite boyhood hobby. He picked up a red one and spun the yarn tightly between the circular wooden discs.

He had spent many days inside these four walls, practising his skills and hoping for someone to show them to. He held the yo-yo tight in his hand before letting it fall to the ground and bouncing it back up easily. His tricks had been numerous, all learned from a book he had got as a gift from his father. He knew now that his father's secretary had probably chosen it, but at the time he had taken it as a challenge to impress the old man. And, as he did with most tasks, he'd poured his heart and soul into it.

In a way he was no different from the little boy who had captured his wife's attention. Leo might not have been an orphan, but he knew what it meant to crave a connection. He had that with Dara now—he felt the completeness that came from the love of a good woman. He had poured all his efforts into creating a life together with his beautiful wife.

Since meeting Dara he had slowly lost interest in the party scene—except for when he opened up a new club. As a bachelor, he had spent his leisure time mainly involved in drinking too much and buying the fastest cars. He'd had no difficulty living in hotels for months at a time. He hadn't known what it meant to have a home.

Dara had shown him just how fulfilling life could be. But now he got the feeling that she felt their life was lacking somehow. If she was happy, why was she escaping to Syracuse every chance she could get?

An image of the longing in her eyes when she spoke about the child there filled his mind. It was suddenly blindingly clear that Dara had developed a newfound yearning for motherhood. And somehow that yearning wasn't something she felt comfortable sharing with him. The thought jarred him, leaving an uncomfortable knot in his stomach.

Leo ran a hand through his hair and threw the yo-yo back into the box. He had never once questioned Dara's steadfast opinion on family. She had made it clear that she would never have children, and that had suited them both. The idea of fatherhood had never been something he aspired to. His own father had been a spectre in his life—one who had drifted in and out, leaving him uncertain and confused. As an adult he had never once considered the idea of starting a family of his own.

But lately he had begun to grow tired of the constant

travelling. These days the only place he wanted to be was here, with his wife, in their true home. He had wanted to say that to her last night, but they had got sidetracked.

He walked back to the *castello* just as evening was setting in and found Dara waiting for him in the kitchen. A bottle of vintage Prosecco sat on the table, two glasses beside it.

'I'm sorry I took so long.' She winced, pouring him a generous glass of wine.

Leo took a sip, appreciating the taste for a moment before shrugging. 'You have a business to run, *carina*. I have to accept that I can never have you all to myself.'

'I've turned my phone off for the evening, so I am one hundred per cent yours. No distractions.' She smiled, pressing her mouth to his.

Leo held her at arm's length, noticing the shadows under her eyes. 'Good. Because I'd like to continue our discussion from last night.'

Dara removed herself from his arms, turning to take a long gulp from her own glass. 'I'd rather we just leave that, actually. I must have been overtired and emotional.'

Her laugh didn't fool him. 'Dara, are you unhappy?' he asked, and watched her face snap up with alarm.

'Why on earth would you think that?'

'You seem...unfulfilled, somehow. These trips to Syracuse tell me that perhaps you might have changed your mind about some things.'

Dara looked momentarily miserable, her expression filled with intense sadness before shifting back to a mask of calm. Anyone else might not have noticed, but Leo knew her better than anyone.

'It's nothing that I plan to act on,' she said coldly. 'There's no need for you to worry.'

'Why would I worry? We are husband and wife, Dara.

We make these kinds of choices together. Maybe I should go with you to Syracuse so you can help me to understand.'

'That's definitely *not* what I want,' Dara snapped.

'*Per l'amore di Dio.*' Leo sucked in a breath to control his frustration. 'Dara, for God's sake, what *do* you want?' he shouted harshly, feeling instant remorse as she flinched.

They stood in silence for a moment, toe to toe in the silence of the kitchen.

'I won't be shouted at.' Dara spoke quietly. 'I need some time alone. I'll see you at dinner.'

She practically ran from the room. Ran away from him.

Leo frowned, looking out of the window at the waves crashing against the cliffs. He had lost his temper—but could she blame him? He was her *husband*, and yet she was determined to battle whatever was bothering her alone. He had a right to know what this was about.

Clearly the answer lay in Syracuse. If she wouldn't go with him, then he would have to go alone.

Dara awoke to a note on her pillow from Leo, telling her that he had some business to attend to and that he would return by the afternoon. His words were plain and to the point, with none of the flowery terms of affection that they usually used. She felt a pang of hurt that he hadn't woken her before leaving, and now she faced a day in the *castello* alone with her thoughts.

She had been hostile and unfair last night. And now she had driven a wedge between them. She sighed, falling back onto the soft Egyptian cotton bedspread, and stared up at the ceiling.

It wasn't that she didn't *want* to share her inner turmoil with her husband. She just felt that it was pointless to do so. Yes, she had formed a bond with Luca. Yes, for the first time in her life she had felt the all-encompassing yearning to care for a child as her own. But she would never do it. She would never be so naive as to assume that she was in any way qualified to be a parent. She was a very good wedding planner, and she hoped she was a satisfying wife. But she was not cut out to be somebody's mother.

Her own mother had been warm and caring. She had given up her career in hotel management to stay at home as a full-time parent and had made it clear that she believed all women should do the same. Dara knew that Leo didn't think that way—he went out of his way to promote equality in his company, and often commented on how proud he was of his wife's accomplishments. And yet the image of her mother baking in the kitchen would always be her measure of what a good wife looked like.

She stared out at the waves crashing onto the cliffs below. Why was she having all these thoughts now? She *loved* her life. She had more than most women could dream of.

Needing to escape her overactive thoughts, she walked to the window. The winds were too high today to walk down on the beach, and being outside in the chilly December air wasn't her idea of a relaxing getaway.

It had been Leo's idea to take time off work, and yet here he was abandoning her on their third day. Clearly he was annoyed, and was choosing to punish her.

Her mind wandered back to the orphanage once more. She was restless and annoyed with herself for allowing this charade to go on for so long. It wasn't fair to the little boy or to the hopeful orphanage staff. She needed to explain herself and give them a clear idea that she would no longer be visiting.

She could see Luca one last time.

Before she'd even realized what she was doing, she'd picked up her car keys and was powering up the cobbled driveway in her Porsche. She could be at the orphanage within the hour, and back well before lunchtime. Leo wouldn't even know she'd gone anywhere.

The familiar white stucco facade of the orphanage was like a balm to the uncomfortable ache in her chest. Dara knocked on the door and stepped back when it swung open to reveal the kind-faced head of the orphanage—Matron Anna.

'Signora Valente, I'm surprised to see you here.' She frowned. 'I thought you were in Palermo this week?'

'What would make you think that?' Dara smiled as she stepped inside and let the younger woman take her jacket.

'Signor Valente said that you were so busy this week...'

'He did? When were you speaking with him?' Dara frowned, just as a roar of laughter came from the nearby common room. A familiar voice drifted down the hall-way—a deep male voice filled with mischief and laughter.

Dara moved silently towards the doorway of the common room, her heart hammering uncomfortably in her chest. The children were all gathered in the centre of the room, on the floor, and each of their little faces was beaming up at the man who stood in the centre of their circle. Leo stood poised with a red yo-yo in his hand. His posture was like that of a magician about to wow his crowd.

'And now for my next trick...' he proclaimed, waiting a moment as the children shouted loudly for him to continue. 'This one is called the lindy loop. Are you ready?'

The excitement in the air was palpable, and every eye in the room was trained on Leo as he set the red object on an intricate movement up in the air. The yo-yo caught several times on its string, before spinning up into the air and down to the ground and then landing safely back into its master's hand.

The children clapped loudly, shouting multiple requests for new tricks at their entertainer. Leo was calm and indulgent, chatting easily to the crowd of little people in a way Dara had never seemed to master. She had spent weeks trying to gain the confidence of these kids, and the most she'd managed had been sharing lunch at the same table.

Luca always stayed by her side, though.

Her thoughts back on the present moment, she suddenly absorbed the fact that her husband was *here*. In the orphanage. He had lied to her, and for that she should be furious.

And yet all she felt was a same sense of anticipation. As if she was hurtling head first down a hill and she had no power to stop it.

As she watched, Luca stepped forward from the crowd of children. His soft black curls were falling forward into his eyes as they always did. He had the kind of unruly hair that refused to behave under the ministrations of any brush. She imagined Leo's hair would be much the same if he let it grow any longer.

Catching her thoughts, she shook her head and watched as her husband sank down to his knees to listen to the young boy whisper something into his ear. Leo listened intently for a moment, before breaking into a huge grin. Luca smiled up at him and they both laughed together at their secret joke.

And Dara felt her heart break completely.

Turning from the door, she walked quickly down the corridor and out to her car. The drive home passed in a blur. Her body felt numb and her insides shook violently.

Once she reached the familiar facade of the *castello*, she walked to the stone wall that overlooked the famous cliffs of Monterocca. And only then did she let the tears come. Great racking sobs escaped her throat and sent violent tremors through her.

It was unthinkably cruel that Leo should look so perfect surrounded by children. The one thing that she could never give him. She wept for the children she would never bear. The children she had denied wanting for so long.

Soon the sound of tyres squealing down the driveway interrupted her silence. Heavy steps were moving fast across the courtyard towards her.

Dara turned just as Leo came to a stop. 'Where have you been?' she asked innocently.

'You know where,' Leo gritted. 'They told me that you arrived and then left—driving like a mad woman.'

'You lied to me,' Dara said, her voice almost a whisper.

'I needed to understand.' He stood with his arms crossed.

'And *do* you? Do you understand now why it was so selfish of me to get so attached?'

'To tell the truth, Dara, no—I don't.' He sighed. 'You keep saying you've been selfish. But I don't understand how you can consider giving your time and attention to those children as selfishness.'

'I wasn't *giving* anything, Leo. I was taking. I got too close. I let Luca get attached to me because it made me feel…needed.' She took a deep shuddering breath, shaking her head at her own foolishness. 'It made me feel like— like I was his mother.' She bit her lip. 'Can't you see how wrong that is? I've given him hope for something that can never happen.'

'What makes you believe that it can never happen, Dara?'

'Look at me, for goodness' sake. I'm a control freak who works crazy hours and spends half the year travelling around the world with my nightclub magnate former playboy husband.'

'That's…quite a mouthful.' Leo's brows rose.

'It's the truth.' She shrugged. 'We're not family people. Aside from the fact that we can never have our own biological children.'

Leo walked past her to the ancient stone boundary wall, leaning over to peer down at the rough sea below them. 'I might be a jet-setting former playboy, but I think I would be ten times the father that mine was.'

Dara froze. 'Leo, I didn't mean that you wouldn't make a great father. Of course you would. You're easy-going and kind. You're reliable and intelligent. You would be amazing.' She shook her head. 'But you're married to *me*.'

'Dara, if it wasn't for you I would still be going through life without a true purpose. Falling in love with you made me realize what is truly important in life. Three years ago if you had told me that I would want to spend the rest of my life living in this castle I would have laughed you out of the room.' He turned to her, taking both of her hands in his. 'But here I am. And this is the only place I want to be.'

'I can't be somebody's mother. I just can't.'

'Dara, did you ever stop and think that maybe it's okay not to be the perfect mother? Sometimes it's okay just to try your best. I mean, you're telling me that you're a workaholic, and yet the matron told me that you've been visiting the orphanage three times a week. That's a two-hour round trip, alone, while simultaneously running your own business, yes?'

Dara shrugged. 'I made the time.'

'Exactly. Because you care about this boy.' Leo stepped forward, grasping her hands in his. 'Dara, I went to that orphanage today because I wanted to understand you. So that I could make you happy.' He paused for a moment. 'I honestly had no idea of the effect it would have on me. I suppose that somewhere in the back of my mind I've always worried that being raised by parents like mine meant that I could never be a good parent myself.'

'You would make a wonderful father, Leo,' Dara said softly.

'I'm not so sure about *wonderful*. But after today I know I would like the opportunity to try.'

Dara looked up into her husband's eyes and saw the emotion there. 'Are you saying that you want us to start a family together?'

'We've been a family from the moment you agreed to spend the rest of your life as my wife. I want to take this next step with you—to start a new adventure.'

Dara closed her eyes, letting the air finally whoosh into her lungs. The fear of even daring to want this had stopped her from acknowledging her true feelings about Luca. Hearing Leo say these things… Hearing him shine a proverbial light on her deepest yearnings…

She looked up at her husband once more and saw that he was watching her quietly.

'I want to be Luca's mother.'

The words came out rushed and tumbled over each other on their way. But once she had said them out loud it was as though she truly understood herself for the first time. Her hands started to shake—a quake that continued up her arms and down into her abdomen.

Leo put his arms around her but she gently removed them, needing to pace for a moment with this newfound sense of terror coursing through her. It was one thing to be afraid of wanting something that she knew could never happen. But to admit that she wanted it…? To open herself to rejection and heartbreak…?

To Leo this was a new feeling—the idea of becoming a

parent. But for Dara this was a sensation that had haunted her for years, a thought that had consumed her at times. She had fought back against the feelings of hopelessness by cutting the thought out of her life altogether and deciding that she no longer wanted to become a mother.

Now she knew the truth. She had never stopped wanting it. She had just been waiting for this moment.

'I can't believe this is happening...' Dara breathed, her thoughts swimming with the enormity of what they were discussing.

'It's only happening if you want it to.' Leo stood in front of her. 'I meant what I said on that beach three years ago. You will always be enough for me, Dara. You are more than I deserve.'

Dara felt the fear melt away as Leo's arms enveloped her, and all her worries seemed smaller all of a sudden. She breathed in the familiar scent of his aftershave and told herself that she needed to commit this perfect moment to memory.

'I want to start a family with you.' She pulled back to look into her husband's eyes. 'I want us to become Luca's parents. If he'll have us, that is.'

'Hearing him speak about you today, I have no doubt that he thinks just as much of you as you do of him,' Leo assured her.

'I hope so.' Dara bit her lip. 'Leo, once we take this step there is no going back. There will be no more impromptu trips to Paris—no more yachting for weeks along the Riviera. We'll have to consider school term times. It won't be just you and I.'

'I'm quite aware that children are a lot of responsibility.'

'I just want to make sure that you're certain this is

what you want. That we aren't going into this with our eyes closed.'

'Dara, stop worrying and let yourself enjoy this. I have complete faith that you will plan every little detail perfectly. Just leave all the fun stuff to me.' He laughed.

Dara smiled. He was right—she was a ball of nerves. She took a deep breath, feeling a sense of excited anticipation hum through her veins.

'I will start proceedings in the morning.' Leo smiled. 'We can go to the orphanage ourselves.'

'I can hardly believe that this is happening.' Dara shook her head. 'Never in my wildest dreams...'

Leo pressed his lips tenderly to hers, his hands spanning her waist and pulling her to him in a tight embrace. 'I was afraid to share you with anyone else, but now I find myself wanting to show you off to the world. You amaze me with all you've overcome.'

'You're the one who helped me to overcome it.'

Their kiss turned from soft to heated, and the wind whipped around them as the sun dipped slowly towards the sea.

The next morning Dara arrived at the orphanage bright and early, with her husband by her side. They entered the common room just as the children had finished breakfast. No sooner had they stepped into the room than a tiny head of jet-black curls came barrelling towards them.

'Do you know the yo-yo man?'

Luca's eyes widened as he looked from Dara to Leo. Dara imagined her husband must look like a giant from the small boy's height, and yet he wasn't frightened.

'Luca, this is my husband Leo. He came here to meet you.'

The other children had filtered into the room, all their

attention on the man with the yo-yo. Leo continued to delight the children with more tricks and Luca sat resolutely by his side, telling all the other children that 'the yo-yo man' had come to meet him.

Before they knew it, the children were called to have lunch. As much as Dara wanted to stay there all day, she knew that now it was time for the official part of their visit.

As the lunch bell rang Luca's eyes turned wide and he ran to her. He looked up at her with that uncertain expression she had come to recognise so well after more than three months of visits.

'I promise that I will come back,' she said solemnly.

Luca was a child of abandonment, so he regularly made her promise that she was coming back in their same special way. Dara held out her pinkie finger, letting him lock it with his own tiny one.

She felt a hand at her waist. Leo stood by her side, watching the exchange with interest. 'Is this some secret handshake I don't know about?' he joked.

'I can teach it to you too,' Luca said quietly.

As Dara watched, her husband got down on his knees and promised the young boy that he would return. She felt a swell of love for this man who had helped her to overcome so much.

Leo straightened, and they waved as the boys ran in single file towards the lunchroom. Luca was the smallest of the lot.

'It was so good of you both to visit us today.' The friendly matron smiled as she welcomed them into her office. 'I couldn't help but notice your interest in little Luca,' she said speculatively.

Dara turned to the woman, meeting her gaze. 'My visits here haven't been as selfless as I've made them out to be.'

'You are a very kind woman, Dara. I don't believe that you came here out of your own interests.'

'Maybe not at first, but it has definitely become that way.'

'I have watched your progress with Luca intently. You know his history. He came to us a very scared and lonely boy. Since your visits he has changed. He talks more with the other children…he is more confident. Your attention did that for him.' She smiled again.

Leo stepped forward, taking Dara's trembling hand in his own. 'My wife and I would like to start proceedings to adopt Luca.' He felt the enormity of the words as he spoke them.

The other woman's eyes lit up with emotion and joy. 'Oh, after yesterday and today I confess that I had started to hope. But our hopes get dashed here far too often.'

'Our intentions are genuine. We would like to become Luca's parents,' Dara said. 'We know that the process is long, but we believe he will be happy with us. That we can give him a good home.'

Tears filled the old matron's eyes as she took one of Dara's hands in her own. 'You have no idea how long I've been waiting for you to realise that, Signora Valente.'

Dara stood by the fireplace, straightening the stockings and biting her lip. Was she jumping the gun by adding one smaller stocking beside their own two? She worried at her bottom lip for a moment, before making a final sweep of the living room. Piles of gifts lay stacked under the tree, ready to be torn open by eager little hands. She had wrapped each box painstakingly in bright paper with intricate bows. She wanted to make today as special as it could possibly be.

'Dara, stop worrying. The place looks amazing.' Leo strode into the living room, his hair lightly ruffled from being outside. 'You're going to have to get used to less organisation around here.'

'I know. I'm just keeping busy.' She sighed.

'He'll be here soon. You'll be kept *very* busy for the weekend. Last chance… You're sure you don't want to hire a nanny?' He smiled mischievously.

'We will do just fine on our own.' Dara laughed as Leo swept her into his arms. 'He's just one little boy—how much work could he be?'

'I have a feeling those are brave last words.'

She felt the excitement and the nerves coursing through him just as they did inside her. Leo pressed his mouth to hers softly, tracing the outline of her lips with own. She twined her fingers in the hair at the nape of his neck and sighed as he deepened the kiss, moulding his hands tightly to her waist. He shaped his body closely against hers, the warmth of him pressing hard against her.

She wanted to remember this moment for ever. Kissing the man she loved, here, in the home they had created, as they waited to welcome their son to his new home for the first time.

Their son.

In just a few moments she would officially be a mother. The realisation hit her like a freight train and she broke off their kiss just as the doorbell rang.

'Are you ready?'

Leo looked into her eyes, squeezing her hand tightly as they made their way to the entrance of the *castello*.

He smiled. 'I can't wait to see his face once he realises he's going to live in a real-life castle.'

Dara felt her nerves melt away as she saw the excited expression on Leo's face. Suddenly she just knew that everything was going to be wonderful from this moment on.

They opened the door to find their social worker helping Luca out of the car. His tiny face was turned up and he was looking at the *castello* with awe.

Dara ushered Luca inside, welcoming the social worker, who would be staying for the settling-in period. The adoption process had definitely been speeded up by Leo, with the Valente name seeming to cut through some of the red tape, but it was far from over. This weekend was for Luca—to ensure that he was happy to come and live with them at the *castello* for good. They had a multitude of activities planned and had put the finishing touches to his bedroom.

Over the past weeks they had spent long hours bonding with the young boy, going on day trips and meeting with various officials. It was a gruelling process, but one that was vital. Everyone had to be sure that he was happy to be adopted by them. That was what mattered most.

Luca ran into the hall and barrelled into Leo's arms. 'Wow, you really *do* live in a castle!'

'I don't tell lies.' Leo smiled down at him.

'Will we be living here all the time?' he asked Dara in a small voice.

Dara looked at the social worker, aware that her every move was being assessed. 'If you would like it, this would be our home, yes.' She turned to Leo, feeling her confidence begin to falter.

'Are there ghosts in this castle?' Luca asked suddenly.

'There used to be.' Leo looked pointedly at Dara for a moment. 'But then a brave princess came and chased all the ghosts away.'

Dara felt tiny fingers wrap around her own. She looked

down to see that Luca had grabbed on to her hand tightly as they ascended the stairs to show him his new bedroom. Her heart soared at this show of affection.

'I thought the knight was supposed to save the princess?' Dara questioned light-heartedly as she gripped her son's hand.

'Sometimes the knight is the one who needs to be saved.'

Leo caught her eye and Dara smiled to herself.

They had saved one another. Two broken souls who had somehow managed to make each other whole again. After all they had overcome in both their pasts, she was certain that the future could only be bright.

* * * * *

If you enjoyed Dara and Leo's story, you can find out where it all started in
RESISTING THE SICILIAN PLAYBOY
*By Amanda Cinelli
available October 2015 wherever
Harlequin Presents books and ebooks are sold.*
www.Harlequin.com

Available October 20, 2015

#3377 A CHRISTMAS VOW OF SEDUCTION
Princes of Petras
by Maisey Yates

With one band of gold, Prince Andres of Petras can erase his past—and most pleasurable—sins. But his prospective bride is untamable Princess Zara. So the playboy prince must seduce her into compliance and crown her by Christmas!

#3378 THE SHEIKH'S CHRISTMAS CONQUEST
The Bond of Billionaires
by Sharon Kendrick

As the snow falls, innocent Olivia Miller finds a darkly handsome and compelling man on her doorstep. The sheikh she refused has arrived to whisk her off to his kingdom...and this time he *won't* take no for an answer!

#3379 UNWRAPPING THE CASTELLI SECRET
Secret Heirs of Billionaires
by Caitlin Crews

Lily Holloway turned her back on the forbidden passion she shared with Rafael Castelli five years ago. But when their paths cross again, Lily attempts to veil herself with deception in order to retain her freedom...and her child!

#3380 A MARRIAGE FIT FOR A SINNER
Seven Sexy Sins
by Maya Blake

Zaccheo Giordano is a man with one thing on his mind: revenge. And he'll start with his ex-fiancée, Eva Pennington. She *will* wear Zaccheo's ring again and he'll ensure their marriage will be real in *every* sense...

HPCNM1015RA

#3381 LARENZO'S CHRISTMAS BABY
One Night With Consequences
by Kate Hewitt
After two years behind bars, Larenzo Cavelli is determined to get his life back...starting with Emma Leighton. It was deception that imprisoned him, so what will happen when he discovers Emma's secret? One he might never be able to forgive...

#3382 BRAZILIAN'S NINE MONTHS' NOTICE
Hot Brazilian Nights!
by Susan Stephens
Chambermaid Emma Fane thinks her best friend's wedding will be the perfect distraction...until she spies Lucas Marcelos—father to her unborn child! It only took one night to change their lives, now they have nine months to face the consequences.

#3383 SHACKLED TO THE SHEIKH
Desert Brothers
by Trish Morey
Nanny Tora Burgess eagerly waits to meet her new boss—but is horrified to discover he's her red-hot, one-night lover! Rashid is cold, distant and has a shocking proposal that will shackle her to the sheikh forever!

#3384 BOUGHT FOR HER INNOCENCE
Greek Tycoons Tamed
by Tara Pammi
Jasmine Douglas is the only one who knows the darkness of Dmitri Karegas's past. But only Dmitri can help when she's forced to put her virginity up for sale. Now he must decide what to do with her...and her innocence!

REQUEST YOUR FREE BOOKS!

HARLEQUIN
Presents

2 FREE NOVELS PLUS
2 FREE GIFTS!

PASSION
GUARANTEED
SEDUCTION

YES! Please send me 2 FREE Harlequin Presents® novels and my 2 FREE gifts (gifts are worth about $10). After receiving them, if I don't wish to receive any more books, I can return the shipping statement marked "cancel." If I don't cancel, I will receive 6 brand-new novels every month and be billed just $4.30 per book in the U.S. or $5.24 per book in Canada. That's a saving of at least 13% off the cover price! It's quite a bargain! Shipping and handling is just 50¢ per book in the U.S. and 75¢ per book in Canada.* I understand that accepting the 2 free books and gifts places me under no obligation to buy anything. I can always return a shipment and cancel at any time. Even if I never buy another book, the two free books and gifts are mine to keep forever.

106/306 HDN GHRP

Name	
	(PLEASE PRINT)

Address		Apt. #

City	State/Prov.	Zip/Postal Code

Signature (if under 18, a parent or guardian must sign)

Mail to the **Reader Service:**
IN U.S.A.: P.O. Box 1867, Buffalo, NY 14240-1867
IN CANADA: P.O. Box 609, Fort Erie, Ontario L2A 5X3

**Are you a current subscriber to Harlequin Presents® books
and want to receive the larger-print edition?
Call 1-800-873-8635 or visit www.ReaderService.com.**

* Terms and prices subject to change without notice. Prices do not include applicable taxes. Sales tax applicable in N.Y. Canadian residents will be charged applicable taxes. Offer not valid in Quebec. This offer is limited to one order per household. Not valid for current subscribers to Harlequin Presents books. All orders subject to credit approval. Credit or debit balances in a customer's account(s) may be offset by any other outstanding balance owed by or to the customer. Please allow 4 to 6 weeks for delivery. Offer available while quantities last.

Your Privacy—The Reader Service is committed to protecting your privacy. Our Privacy Policy is available online at www.ReaderService.com or upon request from the Reader Service.

We make a portion of our mailing list available to reputable third parties that offer products we believe may interest you. If you prefer that we not exchange your name with third parties, or if you wish to clarify or modify your communication preferences, please visit us at www.ReaderService.com/consumerschoice or write to us at Reader Service Preference Service, P.O. Box 9062, Buffalo, NY 14240-9062. Include your complete name and address.

She looked down, caught the glitter of her engagement
ring on the hand that was squeezing him. Then she looked
back up at his face. A mistake.

She barely had a chance to register the hot, angry glitter in his dark eyes before he closed the distance between
them, his mouth crashing down onto hers.

The force of him pushing her back against the wall
crushed their bodies together as he angled his head and
slipped his tongue between her lips.

He proved then what he'd said before. He had the
power. She could do nothing, not in this moment. Nothing but simply surrender to the heat coursing through her,
to the electrical current crackling over her skin with a
kind of intensity she'd never even imagined existed.

His hands were firm and sure on her hips, his body
pressing her to the wall as he sought restitution for her
attempt at claiming control.

"You want a fight?" He growled the words against her mouth. "I can give you a fight, Princess. We don't have to do this the easy way." He angled his head, parting his lips from hers, kissing her neck. She shivered, fear and arousal warring for pride of place inside her. "But if you want to test me, you have to be prepared for the results. I do not know what manner of man you have been exposed to in the past, but I am not one that can be easily manipulated."

He rocked his hips against hers, showing her full evidence of the effect she was having on his body. She had spent so much of her life being ignored that eliciting such a powerful response from such a man gratified her in ways she never could have anticipated.

She didn't know a kiss could be so many different things. That it could serve so many purposes. That it could make her feel hot, cold, afraid, enraptured. But it did. It was everything, and nothing she should ever have allowed to happen between them.

Don't miss
A CHRISTMAS VOW OF SEDUCTION
by USA TODAY *bestselling author Maisey Yates,*
available November 2015 wherever
Harlequin Presents® books and ebooks are sold.

www.Harlequin.com